"The man gave me seventy-two hours to come up with the paintings."

"And if you can't?" Joe asked.

"I don't know, but they're clearly not playing games." Talia glanced back at the photos. "I also called Thomas's mother. I described the paintings and she thinks she remembers seeing them. If she does still have them, they're probably somewhere in their apartment."

Joe started to touch her arm, then pulled back from the too intimate gesture, wishing Talia didn't look so vulnerable. He knew what it was like to have the life of a sibling threatened. Knew what it was like to lose a brother. And personal or not, he would see that neither she nor her sister were hurt.

"I'm going to make sure we find those paintings, and that nothing happens to either one of you in the meantime."

"You can't guarantee that."

"Maybe not." He pulled out his phone, hating the fact that she was right. "But I can promise I'll do everything in my power to stop whoever's behind this."

Lisa Harris is a Christy Award winner and winner of the Best Inspirational Suspense Novel for 2011 from *RT Book Reviews*. She and her family are missionaries in southern Africa. When she's not working she loves hanging out with her family, cooking different ethnic dishes, photography and heading into the African bush on safari. For more information about her books and life in Africa, visit her website at lisaharriswrites.com.

Books by Lisa Harris

Love Inspired Suspense

Final Deposit
Stolen Identity
Deadly Safari
Taken
Desperate Escape
Desert Secrets
Fatal Cover-Up

FATAL COVER-UP

LISA HARRIS

HARLEQUIN® LOVE INSPIRED® SUSPENSE

Recycling programs
for this product may
not exist in your area.

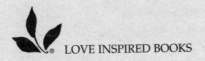

LOVE INSPIRED BOOKS

ISBN-13: 978-0-373-67835-8

Fatal Cover-Up

Copyright © 2017 by Lisa Harris

www.Harlequin.com

Printed in U.S.A.

For He gives His sunlight to both the evil and the good,
and He sends rain on the just and the unjust alike.

—Matthew 5:45

To my kids. I'll never forget our own Italian adventure. Famous landmarks, cross-country train rides, gelato, scorching heat, more gelato...

ONE

Talia Morello stared out across Rome's ancient Colosseum, unable to shake the uneasiness she'd felt all afternoon. Someone was watching her. The hairs on the back of her neck stood up as she glanced around the massive stone amphitheater with its iconic vaulted arches. Drawing in a steadying breath, she told herself she was simply being paranoid. But no matter how hard she tried, she couldn't shake the eerie feeling.

She wiped off a row of sweat from her forehead. Of course, it was impossible to know for certain if someone really was watching her. Four million tourists visited this historical monument every year, and today, even with the steamy July heat, the Colosseum seemed busier than normal, with its never-ending lines snaking around the outside of the monument.

She lifted the bright orange flag she was

carrying a few inches higher to ensure the fifteen enthusiastic tourists who had shown up in the heart of Rome to visit the famous site didn't get separated from her in the crowd. It was her job to see that they left having experienced the best tour of the ruins—even if dismissing the feeling that someone was watching her was proving impossible.

She studied the crowd as she led them toward the last stop of the tour. Someone from a group of Japanese tourists was holding up a selfie stick for a photo. A small crowd clustered together at one of the open spaces overlooking the floor of the Colosseum. Her attention shifted to a man standing against one of the stone walls to the left. He wasn't a part of the group, and didn't seem to be paying attention to his surroundings. Had she seen him before today? Normally, she wouldn't have given him more than a passing glance, but while most of the tourists had cameras or cell phones to take photos, he didn't. A second later he smiled and hurried toward to a woman holding on to two little girls.

Talia swallowed hard. She was just being paranoid. The text she'd received last night was nothing more than a coincidence. A wrong number.

Except she knew that wasn't true.

I know you have the paintings. Meet me at the Spanish Steps when you get off work. I know who murdered your husband. You don't want to be next.

Her heart pounded. While she didn't know about any paintings, the mention of her husband's murder proved this was no coincidence.

"Were all the gladiators slaves?" A twelve-year-old wearing a baseball cap and a New York Yankees shirt pressed in beside her.

"Slaves?" she asked. The boy's question yanked her away from Thomas's death and back to the present. She pasted on a smile as the group kept walking. "No. Actually, some of them were ex-fighters, knights, or they could be anyone drawn in by the roaring approval of the crowd and the hopes of winning. And no," she said before he had a chance to pose the frequently asked question, "they didn't always fight to the death."

Talia shifted the strap of her bag higher on her shoulder, then proceeded to answer another dozen questions as they walked through the amphitheater that had once held seating for the more than 50,000 spectators. Centuries ago, it would have been tightly packed, much like today, as spectators flocked to watch gladiatorial combats, hunts and wild animal fights, and at times even mock naval battle. But focusing on the Colosseum's rich history was proving impossible.

She glanced at her watch. Another five minutes and she'd be done for the day. On a normal Monday, she might have plans to meet a friend for dinner. Today, all she wanted to do was escape back to her apartment and forget about the sinister message. Except she knew she wasn't going to be able to dismiss it that easily.

I know who murdered your husband.

The words played over again through her mind. But it was more than Thomas's unsolved death that haunted her. He'd been shot during a drug raid, with stolen goods found in his possession. He'd been buried three days later in disgrace. And Talia had been left feeling betrayed by the man she loved. They'd promised to love and honor each other, and she'd meant every word of her vows. But instead he'd dishonored her with his crimes.

As soon as the last question from one of the tourists had been answered and she'd thanked them for coming, she let out a sigh of relief and headed for the exit. She drew in a deep breath, trying to calm her nerves. Normally she loved exploring the history of Rome's landmarks, but not today. Today, the thick walls seemed to close in on her as she pressed through the crowded walkways.

And she still had yet to decide her next move.

She slipped on her sunglasses and hesitated outside the exit, knowing she had three choices. She could go to the police, but what could they do? It wasn't as if an actual crime had been committed. Not yet. And on top of that, she'd found out the hard way that you couldn't always trust those sworn to protect.

Her second option was to follow the demands of the message and head toward the Spanish Steps, an option that made her even more nervous than going to the authorities. What happened when they realized she didn't have what they wanted? That was why her best choice seemed to be to ignore the message and go home. She started walking again. In less than five minutes she could be sitting on the subway. In another fifteen she could be in her apartment, lost in a good book on her balcony while trying to forget everything she'd left behind three years ago.

Talia stepped over a crack in the cobble-stone walkway as waves of memories flooded through her. As much as she wanted to simply hide, she knew she'd never be able to just ignore the message. The local police department back in the States had never found Thomas's killer, but neither had she ever heard of any paintings involved in his case. What was the connection of these art pieces to Thomas's death? How had they found her, and why, after all these years, did someone think she had them? And how was it possible for whoever sent the message to know something the police had never discovered?

The string of questions unnerved her. She glanced toward the subway station that would take her to the Spanish Steps and hesitated again. She had the private numbers for both the detective who'd led the investigation into Thomas's death as well as the chief of police he'd worked for. It was still morning in south Texas, so before she contacted the Italian authorities or met with whoever had sent the message, it made sense to talk to the Americans. Decision made, she pressed through the throng of tourists coming and going from the Colosseum toward the subway and home.

A second later, she felt someone rip her bag from her shoulder, then push her down onto the ground. A sharp pain shot up her knee on impact as a man wearing a hooded long-sleeved T-shirt took off down the uneven pathway with her bag. Before she could get up, a second man shouted and took off after the thief.

Someone helped her to her feet. Another person handed her her sunglasses, which had fallen off. She thanked them both as she steadied herself. Her legs felt as if they were about to collapse beneath her. The fear pounding through her wasn't just because she felt violated and vulnerable. Could this incident somehow be related to Thomas's death and the threat she'd received? She managed a breath, then started back down the road, weaving her way once again through the crowd. About a minute later, the man who'd taken off after the thief ran back toward her, carrying her bag.

"Thought you might want this," he said out of breath as he handed over the purse.

"Wow. I can't believe you got it." Her hand shook as she took it from him. "It all happened so fast."

He shot her a smile. "I just happened to be in the right place at the right time."

"And normally I'm the one who tells tourists how to avoid getting robbed."

Except today she'd been the one lost in thought and had become an easy target. "So you're a tour guide." It was more of a state-ment than a question,

"Yeah," she said. "I guess I was distracted today."

She clutched the strap of the bag tighter, distracted by threatening messages and the reminder of her husband's murder. It was no wonder she hadn't even noticed the man.

"Unfortunately the guy who snatched it got away," the man said, "but I saw a couple police officers not too far ahead. If we could come up with a description—"

"No…it's okay." The last thing she wanted to do right now was talk to the police. "Petty theft is an everyday occurrence, and besides, the guy's long gone by now. I'm just thankful to have my bag. Replacing my ID would have been a nightmare."

He shoved his hands into the pockets of his shorts and shrugged. "I'm just happy I could help."

She knew he was American from his ac-cent. Just over six feet tall, he was dressed casually in gray chino shorts, a black T-shirt and a black baseball cap. Dark brown hair, brown eyes and good-looking… Okay, very good-looking. Not that it mattered.

"Are you all right?" His gaze dropped to her knee.

"I think so." She glanced down at the trail of blood on her leg just below the hem of her dress, where she'd scraped it on the rough pavement. "It's nothing. But thank you again. I'm not sure how you were able to get it back, but you really did save me a lot of hassle."

"Not a problem, but hey…" He caught her eyes as she looked up. "Why don't you let me buy you a cup of coffee? It will give you a few minutes to catch your breath and clean up your knee."

"You don't have to do that."

"I know I don't have to, but I'd like to."

She hesitated. Maybe a cup of coffee wouldn't hurt. The diversion would help calm her nerves and right now she definitely needed to calm down.

"I saw a little café just around the corner," he continued, glancing back down the street. "What do you say?"

"Okay." She answered before she'd had a chance to really think about it, then immediately questioned her decision. She'd gone out with a few men since moving here, but never more than once or twice, and certainly not with a stranger. She pushed away the concern. It wasn't like this was a date. He was just a friendly American who'd come to her rescue.

"I never got your name," she said as they sat down at one of the small outside tables at the busy café a minute later. She signaled to the waiter and ordered two espressos in Italian, then pulled out a package of tissues from her bag and started dabbing at her knee.

"Joe Bryant," he said, settling into his chair. "From Virginia."

"Talia Morello, born and raised in Texas, actually," she said.

"For a Texan your Italian is flawless."

"My father was Italian and has family here, so I ended up spending most summers in Italy while I was growing up. What about you, though?" she asked, wanting to shift the conversation away from herself. There were things—personal things—he didn't need to know about her. "Are you here on holiday?"

"The trip's work-related, actually." He pressed his fingers against the table, then pulled out his badge. "I went for the tourist look today, but I actually work for the FBI's art crime team."

"Art crime team?" She glanced at the badge, panic settling in as she repeated his words. This couldn't be another coincidence. She received a message demanding some artwork and now the FBI's art division was here? She searched her brain for a connection, but nothing made sense.

"Listen, I know this is going to sound crazy," he said, breaking into her thoughts, "but I know who you are. I'm actually here because I was hoping for a chance to ask you a few questions about your husband."

The familiar scenery around her began to blur. The line of shops down the avenue sprinkled with tourists, the smell of pizza baking, purple and red flowers wilting in the afternoon sun...

She'd moved to Italy to escape the questions.

"I know he was a police officer," he continued. "I know he was accused of stealing from a number of police raids, that he was murdered and that the murderer was never caught. I know you were even questioned once as to whether or not you were involved—"

"I was cleared of any charges—"

"I know, and I'm not here to accuse you of anything. I've gone through the reports and they clearly show that no evidence ever led back to you."

Not that that fact had stopped the accusations. She bit the inside of her cheek. She'd worked so hard to put Thomas and his murder behind her, along with the shame in discovering he'd been involved in something illegal. And now everything about today was forcing her to dredge it all up again.

"Listen," he said, as the waiter slid two espressos in front of them. "This isn't how I planned to approach you, but it is very important that we talk."

"Agent Bryant—"

"Please…you can call me Joe," he said, handing her a business card with the FBI logo on it along with his name. "I know this isn't easy for you."

"Joe… Thomas died a long time ago." She ran her finger over the card before looking back up at him. "And even though his killer was never found, his case was eventually closed. So unless you have the name of his murderer, I don't know what you could tell me that would matter at this point."

"I don't have that, but what if I told you that some new evidence has surfaced regarding his case?"

New evidence? Was that what all of this was about? A wave of nausea swept through her. There had to be a connection between Agent Bryant—Joe—this recently surfaced information and whoever had sent her that threatening text message.

"What did you discover?" she asked. "More evidence of his guilt?"

If that was what he was talking about, she didn't want to know. Not after all this time. Not after moving to Italy to start a new life, a life without the stigma of his murder and his betrayal. She and Thomas had just celebrated their six-month anniversary days before he'd been murdered. The chief had come to her house personally to tell her what had happened.

"I'm sorry to have to tell you this," he'd said, "but Thomas was shot tonight after a drug bust gone wrong." He'd hesitated from where he'd sat across from her in their living room. "And unfortunately, we have solid proof pointing to the fact that he was involved—possibly for quite some time—in stealing evidence, both money and drugs, from a number of raids."

At that moment, everything she knew and believed about the man she'd fallen in love with had been completely shattered.

"Not more evidence of his guilt," Joe said, adding a packet of sugar to his drink. "But we have found a lead to the person who murdered him."

"I don't understand." Her hands shook as she took a sip of her espresso. "How is the FBI's art crime division connected to Thomas's murder?"

She needed to know. Because if there was new information on the case, she'd have expected to hear the update from Thomas's department. Not the FBI. And while she might want to forget the past, a part of her also needed closure. Which was why as much as she wanted to stand up and walk away, she knew she wouldn't be able to until she heard what he had to say.

Joe took a sip of his espresso before answering her question, knowing that what he needed to tell her was going to be difficult for her to hear. Two days ago, he'd flown across the Atlantic, following a lead, in order to talk with her in person. And yet since his arrival there hadn't seemed to be a right moment or a right way to approach her.

"Three months ago a young man was killed during a museum heist," he began.

She shook her head. "Okay, but what does that have to do with Thomas?"

"Forensics was able to match the bullet that killed him to another murder where the same gun was used. It was the same gun that killed your husband."

He caught the pain in her eyes and took a moment to study her reaction while giving her the time she needed to digest the information he'd just given her. He'd done his homework before catching the flight to Rome, but she looked younger than he'd expected. From her file he'd learned she was twenty-seven. She had a large family on her father's side, but only one sibling, a sister named Shelby who lived in Dallas. Her parents were both deceased.

Today, her dark hair was pulled back in a ponytail with loose wisps around her face. She was pretty in that classic sense, and fit in perfectly as an Italian in her black-and-white dress and wedge sandals. And from what he knew about her so far, she was the kind of woman he'd like to get to know better. Not that he would. He'd gotten involved with a woman once before while working a case, and he'd learned quickly to never mix FBI business with personal relationships.

"Are you okay?" he asked, when she didn't respond.

"I don't know." She stared at her cup. "This was just the last thing I was expecting to hear today."

"So you believe me?" He couldn't exactly blame her hesitation. A complete stranger had walked up to her off the street and started talking to her about her husband's murder.

"Enough to hear you out," she said finally.

He glanced around the crowded café, wishing they were somewhere more private. But at least with the chatter of customers and the sound of cups clinking, no one would be able to listen in on their conversation.

"Okay," he began, "during the recent heist, two paintings worth over two million dollars were stolen. It was the fourth time in the past several years where thieves used a similar pattern. All the works were stolen during the day while the museum was open. And each time they strategically took small pieces of art with high price tags. The difference this time was that one of the guards was killed trying to stop them."

Talia shook her head. "I'm sorry someone was killed, but I still don't understand what this has to do with me or with Thomas. He didn't steal art. He stole drug money and cocaine."

He caught another flicker of pain when she spoke and regretted having her dredge up so much from her past. "When Forensics came up with a match, I went to your husband's department and got your husband's file. Among the case notes, there were three postcard-sized paintings by nineteenth-century Italian artist Augusto Li Fonti logged as a part of Thomas's personal belongings, but they're never mentioned again."

"Three postcards?" Her eyes narrowed as she took a sip of her espresso. "I don't remember any mention of postcards, or understand why that would be significant."

"In the second museum heist we believe to be connected to the case I'm working on now," he continued, "there were three paintings the size of postcards stolen. And because it's not uncommon for the cartel to trade valuable artwork as collateral, it's very possible for something like that to be found at a drug raid. I believe they were at the house where your husband was killed."

She set down her cup. "And you think I have them?"

"You could have them without realizing how valuable they are."

A shadow crossed her face. "There are still people who believe that I knew what my husband was up to. And possibly even helped him."

"Did you?" he asked.

"No…" She hesitated, clearly unsure if she could trust him. "I need to tell you something." It seemed she'd decided she didn't have anyone else to turn to.

"Okay." He waited for her to respond.

She paused one more time then pulled out her phone, clicked on a message and handed it to him. "I received a text message late last night. They told me to bring the three paintings to the Spanish Steps when I got off work. Apparently you're not the only one who believes I have them."

He quickly read through the message. "You were planning to meet them?"

"I can't," she said. "Because I don't have what they want."

"So you don't remember any small paintings or drawings in your husband's personal things?"

"Maybe…I don't know." She pushed a wisp of hair behind her ear. "After the investigation closed, the department gave me a box of his personal things. I spent days sorting through all his stuff. I ended up giving some of his personal things to my mother-in-law, then donated most of the rest." She looked up and caught his gaze. "You have to understand I'd just found out that my husband was a dirty cop and skimming money from police raids. I didn't exactly want to keep reminders of him around."

He understood what she was saying, but now there was something else she needed to know. Someone else—perhaps someone with access to the information he had—had made the same connection to Talia that he'd made. And whoever was after the paintings had killed before. Which meant if that person believed she had them, then her life was in danger.

TWO

Joe watched as Talia rubbed the back of her neck with her fingertips. A part of him understood how she felt. Not only was there a strong possibility that her life was in danger, but she also had to be questioning her past decisions. And going through a long list of what-ifs. It was something he'd done far too much lately. But why wouldn't she? The man she'd given her heart to had betrayed her, and now she was suddenly having to deal with what he'd done all over again.

"Tell me about the paintings they want," she said, taking the last sip of her espresso.

"Do you want another espresso first?" he asked.

"No. I'm fine."

"Okay." He grabbed his phone and pulled up a photo of the three paintings the museum curator had given him, then handing the phone to her. "They were stolen from a museum in Boston four years ago. A trio of paintings worth somewhere around half a million each."

"They're beautiful," she said, studying the seacoast scenes.

"Do you recognize them?"

She turned the phone sideways. "You said they're small?"

"Yes."

"Then maybe. I just never made the connection. When I received the text message, I imagined paintings that hung on the wall, but you said Thomas's list of personal items returned to me included three postcards. It's strange…he used to send me postcards when he traveled."

"So you do remember them."

"I think so, but like I said, I didn't pay much attention at the time to what the department gave me. I just thought they were postcards from one of his trips." She took one last look at the photos, then handed him back the phone. "And apparently whoever passed them on to me assumed the same thing, as well."

"Do you know where they are now?"

"I only wish I did. Because then I'd be standing on the Spanish Steps right now, handing them over to whoever wants them and putting an end to all of this." She shoved her empty cup toward the middle of the table. "You said they use art as collateral."

"Art has the unique advantage of having an international value without the hassle of money laundering and currency conversion."

Talia shook her head. "Meaning?"

"Over the past decade there has been a huge push to regulate money laundering. Organized crime has adapted by using artwork instead of cash, sometimes in everything from drug deals, to tobacco trafficking, to gunrunning. And while the value of a piece of art that is used as currency is far less than its estimated legitimate value, it can still be worth millions."

"So I understand how they ended up in the middle of a cartel meth lab, but here's something that doesn't add up—why now? Why are these paintings being connected to me three years after Thomas's death?"

"I'm not sure, but it seems to have happened after I started looking in to the connection with your husband's case and started asking questions."

"So what are you saying? Someone inside the department is involved in this? Another dirty cop like my husband?" Her eyes widened at the thought. "Maybe even someone who worked with my husband. I mean, who else would know the case has been reopened? Who else would be looking for those paintings?"

"All of that could be true," he said, wishing he had more answers for her. "He might have been working with someone else, or had connections inside, someone who's been waiting all this time for a lead that would uncover the location of the paintings."

"But almost three years have passed." She shook her head. "And you don't know if the gun that killed my husband was sold or stolen."

"True." He hesitated, but he needed to know more from her perspective. "I know this is hard for you, but what do you know about that night? Were there any discrepancies that bothered you after his death?"

"Other than the fact that he was accused of stealing over two hundred thousand dollars in cash and drugs from previous drug raids?" She shook her head. "I never could justify that."

"So you never suspected he was involved in something illegal?" he asked.

"Never. I'd noticed he was distracted, but he'd been working long hours on a couple of tough cases. What I never imagined was that he was stealing evidence. Thomas was good at his job, and I'd always believed he was an honest man, as well." A shadow crossed her face. "But I quickly learned that even those closest to you can hide the darkest secrets."

"So no other inconsistencies?" he asked, not missing the ache in her voice.

"I'm not sure. What are you looking for?"

Joe tapped his foot, knowing he needed to tread carefully. "I'm not sure, actually. I spoke to the chief of police and read the case file. There were things that didn't add up. Holes in the case. And while there had been a number of other instances where drug money had gone missing over the previous year, they were never linked conclusively to Thomas. The only solid evidence against him was what was found on him that night and a bank account with ten thousand dollars in it."

Which meant even though they only had circumstantial evidence, the previous thefts had also been pinned on her husband. How it all related now to his FBI case, he still wasn't sure, but the more information he had, the better the chances of finding what he was looking for.

Talia ran her finger along the edge of the table. "The case was closed quickly. At the time I was grateful, but now..."

"It makes sense. The department would have

wanted to keep an internal scandal quiet and make it go away as quickly as possible."

"Are you implying there's a chance Thomas might have been innocent?"

"I wouldn't jump to any conclusions, and in all honesty, your husband's death isn't my case." He tried to backtrack, but it was already too late. The seed had been planted in her mind. "My job is to find the stolen artwork, return it to the rightful owners and in the process help keep it out of the cartel's hands."

She leaned forward. "But from what you know—with the inconsistencies of the case—is it possible someone was covering something up and framed Thomas?"

"I can't answer that."

Joe finished the last sip of his espresso. He couldn't blame her for grabbing on to the slightest thread of hope that her husband was innocent. That wasn't why he was here. But still…

"Tell me what you were told about the day your husband was murdered."

"His boss came to me the day after Thomas's death with the details. He told me that Thomas and his partner had been called to check on a possible meth house with two other officers." As she spoke, he caught the lack of emotion in her voice. It was as if she was simply a reporter spewing out the news. Not the grieving widow of the victim. "The officers swept the house. No one was there, but it was full of equipment for cooking meth along with a large amount of cash and other stolen goods. Apparently Thomas heard something in the back of the house while they were busy securing the property. The other officers heard a shot. Thomas was dead by the time they found his body. The bullet had gone through his temple, killing him instantly. The back door was open, but they never found who'd killed him. But they did find ten thousand dollars in cash stuffed under his bulletproof vest. Later they discovered other stolen evidence hidden in the trunk of his car, and a bank account that pointed to the fact that this hadn't been the first time."

"I can't imagine what you went through," he said, not missing the pain in her voice.

"They brought me in, wanting to prove I knew what he was doing, which I didn't. They tore our apartment apart from top to bottom, but never found anything."

"You said you gave some of your husband's personal things to your mother-in-law?" If she'd seen the paintings, there had to be a way to trace where they'd gone.

"Yes."

"Do you think she might have them?"

Talia shrugged. "I honestly don't know. I never asked her what she did with his things. Thomas's family lives in Venice, but his parents are out of the country on a cruise right now. I could try to get a hold of them and ask her if she remembers."

He caught the doubt surfacing in her eyes, as if she was trying to decide if she could trust him. And he couldn't blame her.

"Talia, I—"

Her phone went off. She pulled it out of her pocket and clicked on the incoming message. He watched her face go pale as she stared at the screen. She shoved the phone across the table for him to read.

You really should have done what you were told.

He read the message, then scrolled through the two photos that were attached. One was of Thomas's body at the crime scene from the night he'd been murdered. The second was a photo of them sitting at the café.

Fatal Cover-Up

Every fiber of his being was on alert as he glanced around the open café. But looking for someone with a camera was like looking for a specific piece of hay in a haystack. Almost everyone around them was a tourist with either a camera or a cell phone.

"Do you recognize anyone?" he asked. "Maybe the man who tried to swipe your bag."

"I don't know...I don't think so." She shoved back her chair, and slung her bag across her shoulder. "I'm sorry. I need to go."

"Talia, please wait. You don't understand what you're up against—"

"I just need to go."

A second later, she disappeared into the crowd. He grabbed a couple of bills from his wallet, dropped them onto the table and hurried after her.

Talia searched the narrow street as she hurried toward the subway past the row of shops and restaurants and apartment buildings. She shouldn't have left the café, but she wasn't sure she could trust Joe. She wanted to. He seemed an honest man. But so had Thomas until she'd found out the truth about him. Which was why for three years, she'd done everything she knew to put the past behind her and forget. But now suddenly, in the last twenty-four hours every memory and fear she'd had after his death was being dredged up.

I don't want to go back there, God.

Not now. Not ever.

She'd accepted the fact that her husband had betrayed her trust. She'd even accepted his death. But it had completely changed her life, and the way people looked at her. There were those who thought there was no way she didn't know what he'd been involved in. Others simply felt sorry for her. And even though she'd finally healed to the point that she was able to go on with her life, it didn't mean that the familiar apprehensions didn't sometimes rise to the surface.

She wove her way through a group of young people standing at the top of the stairs that led to the underground Metro. She needed to leave, and get away from Rome. But where would she go? She had friends, but she didn't want to get them involved. And the only person here who knew what was going on was Joe Bryant.

But could she rely on him?

She hurried down the stairs toward the subway platform through the throng of commuters waiting to get onto the next train. The ground was scattered with cigarette butts. Advertisements were pasted onto the walls. She quickly stepped into the car before the doors slammed shut, then let out a sharp breath of air. A street musician began playing the accordion in the corner of the crowded space as she grabbed on to the metal pole in order to keep her balance. She should feel safe, but even surrounded by people, she had to fight the urge to run. They were out there somewhere. Watching her. Following her...

A group of students chattered in the corner. A woman bounced a toddler in her lap. A businessman talked loudly on his cell phone. Her surroundings faded and were replaced by memories. The day they told her Thomas was dead. The day she buried him. The day she'd sat in the interrogation room for hour after hour, answering their questions. The police had eventually dismissed the possibility of her involvement, but there had still been lingering questions. How could she not have known? She was, after all, his wife.

She fought to push away the memories. She could go home, pack up a bag and take a train to Naples. Or maybe she'd go across the border into France. But that would only delay the inevitable. Until she found the paintings, and discovered who was after them, this wasn't going to be over. And she wasn't going to find out the truth by running.

The sun had slipped behind a line of clouds by the time she made it to her stop and climbed the long flight of stairs to the street level. She breathed in the smell of freshly baked bread from the bakery nestled beneath her apartment building, wanting to turn back time to yesterday, when everything had felt normal. She'd fallen in love with the area the first time she'd visited. Ivy leaves climbed the sides of the century-old building, with its green shutters and flower boxes. Laundry blew in the breeze on a clothing line on the second story. She glanced at the glass display case in the bakery window. Flaky croissants filled with homemade custard, cannoli and her favorite, chocolate mousse on a chocolate biscuit covered in dark chocolate... She wished she could stop now and consume one; it'd be a stress reliever.

Instead her phone rang. A wave of adrenaline rushed through her as she pulled it out of her pocket. If it was them again...

She checked the caller ID and hesitated.

She recognized the area code. It was someone from Texas. She opened the door to the apartment building and took the call.

"Hello?"

"Talia…it's Captain Blythe."

She started up the narrow flight of stairs to her apartment on the fifth floor. It had been months since she'd heard from the department where her husband had once worked. "I was actually planning to call you today. It's been a long time."

"Yes, it has." There was a pause on the line. "Listen, I felt you needed to know that your husband's case has been reopened. The gun that killed him was involved in another, more recent murder."

Hearing him repeat what Joe had just told her made the situation seem so much more real.

"The FBI's gotten involved," he continued. "There's an agent—"

"Joe Bryant," she said, finishing his sentence. "He's with the FBI and here in Rome. I just met him."

"So you know about the reopened case?"

"Yes," said, starting for the third floor. "Can I trust him?"

"I didn't meet him, but the chief did and was impressed when the guy came by. He believes there were pieces of stolen art at the raid where your husband died, which is the reason the FBI is involved. The bottom line is that maybe after all this time they'll find out who killed Thomas."

She was breathing harder as she took the last flight of stairs to the top floor. This was the closure she'd prayed for. They'd never been able to find the owner of the gun. Never been able to find who'd pulled the trigger and murdered Thomas.

The case is breaking open again, God. I didn't want to go there, but if this ends up helping me put it all behind me for good...

That was what she needed.

"I won't keep you," Captain Blythe said, interrupting her thoughts, "but if you need anything, call me."

She said goodbye and hung up, wondering if she should have told him about the threats. But something had made her hesitate. Joe had implied that his reopening up the case had prompted someone to come after the paintings. But did that mean that someone else—someone inside the department—had been involved in Thomas's death?

She pulled out her key and opened the front door to her apartment loft, trying to make sense of everything. The implications of the matching bullets, the text messages and inconsistencies she'd seen with the case… The man she'd married never would have been involved in stealing evidence, but she'd never been able to get anyone to listen to her. And eventually she'd come to accept that Thomas wasn't the person she'd known all those years.

Inside the one-bedroom apartment, the space was a small, open layout with a cozy terrace and views of the neighboring rooftops and monuments in the distance. But it wasn't the familiar layout of home that caught her attention as she stepped into the room. Someone had been here. Talia felt a sick feeling wash over her, along with a wave of panic. Books had been pulled down from their shelves, red couch cushions and half a dozen throw pillows lay scattered across the hardwood floor, while her artwork had been ripped from the walls. She picked up the shattered glass frame holding the photo of her with her parents and little sister that had been taken before her mom and dad had been killed in a car wreck.

Who had done this?

Wind blew through the open terrace door, causing the white sheer curtains she'd picked up at a local flea market to flutter in the breeze. Something clattered against the floor in the bedroom. She froze beside the kitchen counter. Whoever had trashed her house was still here. Without thinking, she set down the photo, grabbed a butcher knife from the kitchen counter and started for her bedroom.

When she stepped through the doorway, he was going through her dresser—the same man who'd grabbed her bag outside the Colosseum. Her intrusion into the room seemed to startle him for a second, then he pulled a gun out of its holster and pointed it at her.

"You should have shown up with the paintings," he said in English with a thick Italian accent. "Toss me your bag."

She hesitated, then threw it at him, still holding the knife. But the blade would be useless against a man with a loaded gun. He dumped the contents on her bed, scattering them across the dark blue bedspread.

She gripped the handle of the knife between her fingers.

"They're not here," he said, rummaging through her things. "The paintings. Where are they?"

"I don't have them." Talia fought to keep her voice steady. "I never did."

He shook his head as if trying to figure out his next move. Light streamed in from the bedroom window. The man was in his mid-to-late twenties. Brown eyes. Dark hair with a streak of blond across his bangs.

He took a step forward. "I was told you'd say that. You knew you couldn't fence the art right after your husband's death, so you decided to be patient and wait to sell them."

She shook her head. "Who told you that?"

"It doesn't matter. All you need to know is that I wouldn't cross the person I work for. They were involved in the death of your husband, they'll kill again if they have to."

"Over a piece of art?" She pressed her lips together, trying to fight the panic. But that wasn't the only thing that sent a chill through her. He knew who'd killed her husband.

The intruder didn't answer her question. But he didn't have to.

"I don't have them," she repeated.

"And I said I don't believe you. They were in your husband's personal items, which were later given to you by the police."

As he moved to the smaller bedside table, his gun still pointed in her direction, another memory surfaced. A few weeks after Thomas had died someone had broken into their house while she'd been out visiting with a friend. The only things that had been taken were a few pieces of her jewelry. At the time, she'd thought it was nothing more than a random break-in, but now... What if there was another explanation? What if the thief had been looking for something specific, like three valuable paintings?

But she didn't have them. Or did she? Her mind raced. The days after Thomas's death were still a blur, but she'd told Joe the truth. She'd given most of her husband's personal things to her mother-in-law in an attempt to get rid of the memories. And while the paintings Joe had shown her seemed vaguely familiar, she wasn't sure what she might have done with them. Could they really be there?

She eyed the gun that still pointed at her as the attacker continued searching. She needed to get someone's attention. The balcony door to her bedroom was open. She could scream. Mrs. Lamberti from downstairs wouldn't hear her—the woman was almost deaf—but someone else might catch her cry for help.

She started toward the door, but the man shifted at the movement and aimed his gun at her heart. "I want you to drop the knife and don't even think about making a sound."

She hesitated as her options vanished, then let the knife fall against the wood flooring.

Show me what to do, God. Please...

"Here's the deal. If you're lying to me, they will come after you. And in the meantime, I was told you might need some motivation." He pulled an envelope from his back pocket and dropped it on the bed beside him. "I understand that you and your sister are close."

She picked up the envelope and pulled out a handful of black-and-white surveillance photos of her sister. She stared at the shots of Shelby getting into her car at work, pumping gas at the local station, walking her Maltese poodle after school...

No, no, no. This couldn't be happening.

The room began to spin. She couldn't breathe. "You can't do this."

"Except I can." His cocky smile sent a chill down her spine. "And if you really don't have the paintings, you've got seventy-two hours to find them."

THREE

Joe found Talia's name and number on the entry phone next to the doorway of the apartment block. He hesitated, wondering if he should buzz her, then changed his mind as an older woman with an armful of groceries opened the locked lobby building door. He slipped in behind her, then ran up the stairs to the fifth floor.

He paused at an open door on the landing—Talia's door—and his senses automatically shifted to high alert. He'd seen Talia slip into the building ahead of him, which meant she was here. But something wasn't right. He stepped inside. The living room had been trashed, leaving couch cushions, books and photos scattered across the floor.

"Talia?" He crossed the empty room, wishing that the Italian government allowed him to be armed. "Talia?"

A man bolted out of an adjoining room and shoved past Joe, knocking him into the wall. Five foot ten, dark hair with a streak of blond... It was the man from the Colosseum!

He pointed a Glock at Joe as he headed toward the door. "Don't even try and follow me."

Joe shouted again for Talia. He needed to go after the man, but if she was hurt... "Talia? Are you okay?"

She stepped into the doorway of the living room, her face ashen, and nodded.

"Then I'll be back."

Ignoring the man's warning, Joe spun around and strode after him. They needed to get this guy and find out who he was and who he was working with.

God, I need some help here. Both for Talia's sake and for my own.

He needed to know the truth. Joe needed closure—not only in the string of art thefts the FBI was investigating, but also in his personal life.

Shoving back the distracting thoughts and forcing his mind to focus, he ran down the narrow hallway to the stairwell. The sound of the other man's footsteps echoed as Joe flew down the flight of stairs, trying to bridge the gap between them. The door to the front lobby slammed open against the wall below him, then shut.

And he still had two more floors to go.

His heart was racing by the time he made it to street level and stepped outside the structure into the afternoon sunshine. He searched the movement of pedestrians and traffic. The air smelled like fresh bread and chocolate. A car honked. A moped whizzed by as he hurried to the corner, debating which way to go. The intruder had to be here somewhere, but there was no sign of him. And the problem was, he could be anywhere. Joe glanced to his right past the busy intersection lined with stores and restaurants and the occasional bakery. Another two blocks to his left was the subway. Tracking him at this point was going to be impossible.

Irritated, he headed back to the apartment building. He needed to make sure Talia was really okay. A minute later he pressed the number of her apartment, waited for her to buzz him back into the building and headed up again to the fifth floor. His mind worked to sort through the few bits of information he had. Reopening the case had triggered someone to go after the paintings. But who? It had to be someone who believed that at some point Thomas had possession of them. Which led him back to his original theory. Whoever was after the paintings had most likely been there the night Thomas had been murdered.

When Talia opened the apartment door for him, she was on her cell phone. She signaled for him to wait a moment, then turned away, but not before he caught the tears streaming down her cheeks.

"Shelby, as soon as you get this message, call me." She dropped her phone onto the kitchen counter, then caught his gaze. "I'm sorry."

"Hey…it's okay. He's gone." He couldn't blame her for being terrified. It was one thing to have someone snatch your bag in public, but having someone invade the privacy of your home with a weapon was going to take a lot longer to forget. "I'm going to use some of my connections with the Italian police and find a way to track this guy down. We've got a good description—"

"No." She was crying harder now. "It's not okay. He threatened my sister. He's got surveillance photos of her at her house, and at her job…"

"Listen, I know this is hard, but I need you to tell me exactly what happened," he said. "And we will figure this out. I promise."

She grabbed a tissue off the counter. "I can't

get a hold of my sister. If anything happens to Shelby because of this I'll never forgive myself."

"Show me the photos."

He followed her into the bedroom, where she sat down on the edge of the bed and picked up one of the pictures. "There are ones of Shelby outside the school where she works in Dallas, outside her house..."

Joe flipped through the photos, understanding her concern. Someone had killed her husband, and now they'd shown her that they could get to both Talia and her sister.

Joe pulled out his own phone. They needed to find a way to put an end to this. "If you'll give me her address, I'll have someone sent to her place right now. And if she's not there, I'll make sure they track her down and ensure she's okay."

She grabbed a piece of paper and a pen off her desk and started writing down the address. "The man gave me seventy-two hours to come up with the paintings."

"And if you can't?" he asked.

"I don't know, but they're clearly not playing games." She glanced back at the photos. "I also called Thomas's mother. I described the paintings and she thinks she remembers see-

ing them. If she does still have them, the artwork is probably somewhere in my in-laws'
apartment."

He started to touch her arm, then pulled
back at the intimate gesture, wishing she didn't
look so vulnerable. But he knew what it was
like to have the life of a sibling threatened.
Knew what it was like to lose a brother. And
personal or not, he was going to make certain
neither she nor her sister were hurt.

"We're going to find those paintings, and
ensure nothing happens to either one of you
in the meantime."

She blew her nose again. "You can't guarantee that."

"Maybe not." He hated the fact that she was
right. "But I can promise that I'll do everything
in my power to stop whoever's behind this."

While Joe started making calls on his cell
phone, Talia hurried to shut and lock both the
balcony and the front door. Not that closing
up the apartment made her feel safe. A man
had already found a way to break in to her
house. Which meant she wasn't sure she'd
ever feel safe here again. Not only was her
life being threatened, but now her sister was
also potentially in danger. And all because of

some missing paintings She glanced at the clock, then redialed Shelby's number. Texas was seven hours behind Rome, so there was a good possibility she had her phone off while she was teaching, assuming Shelby was okay. She hoped that Joe would be able to keep his promise, and that everything would be fine. But she knew firsthand that sometimes things didn't turn out the way you wanted them to.

Joe talked on his phone while pacing in her living room. There was something surprisingly calming about his presence. But the reality was that he was a complete stranger, and the captain's call had only managed to erase some of her doubts concerning the FBI agent. And yet somehow Joe Bryant was still managing to take the edge off her panic.

She closed her eyes, unable to get rid of the constant flood of memories. Not long after Thomas's death, the chief had given her a box of his personal things. At the time, she'd felt too betrayed to do anything more than glance through the belongings before she got rid of most of what was inside. Thankfully, a friend of hers had advised her not throw away everything that reminded her of him, just because of her strong feelings of betrayal. She'd gone with the advice and had kept a few things, which she'd transferred to a smaller container then mailed the rest in a box to her mother-in-law in Venice.

And then she'd done her best to forget about it. Until now.

She glanced around the small apartment. There was really only one place it could be. She found the small, nondescript box under her bed behind a suitcase.

She lifted off the lid and felt a rush of emotion sweep through her. On the top was their wedding invitation, a black card with white-and-teal print. Beneath that were photos from their honeymoon to Ireland, the watch she'd given him for their first anniversary and their wedding rings. And along with these symbols were everything she'd thought they'd promised each other.

For better, for worse.
For richer, for poorer.
To love and to cherish.
Till death do us part.

She'd worked to put her past behind her, but now everything she'd tried to forget had risen to the surface, making her wonder if she was ever going to be truly free. She dug through the rest of the box until she touched the thin sheet of tissue paper in the very bottom. There were no postcards. No paintings.

"Talia?"

Joe's voice broke into her thoughts and pulled her back into the present.

"I just got off the phone with a friend of mine in Dallas. He's sending out a patrol call to your sister's house right now and promised to tell me as soon as they find her."

She set down the box next to her, hoping it was going to be enough to keep her sister safe. "Thank you."

"I also called a contact of mine here in Italy. He's with the Italian version of the FBI's art crime team, the Carabinieri art squad."

"I think I've heard of them."

"They deal with art theft, damage to monuments and archaeological zones. Anyway, he's promised to help look into the case and see if he might be able to track down our hooded thief."

"He's here in Rome?" she asked.

"He has an office here, but he's currently at an archeological site, doing some monitoring. He's promised to see what he can find out." Joe glanced at the box sitting next to her. "What are you doing now?"

"Looking through the few things I kept after Thomas's death. The paintings aren't here."

Which meant they had to be in Venice.

She stood, then grabbed a backpack from her closet and started packing. She couldn't stay here anyway. Not when they knew where she lived. She could take a train north to Venice. Her mother-in-law might be somewhere basking in the beauty of Scandinavia but Thomas's brother had a key and would let her in.

"Wait a minute," Joe said. "What are you doing?"

"I can get a key to my in-law's house from Thomas's brother. If the paintings are there, I should be able to find them."

"In Venice?"

She nodded.

"Then I'm coming with you."

She dropped a pair of comfy flats into the bag. "You don't have to do that."

"Yes, I do. Your husband was more than likely killed over these paintings, and now both you and your sister have been threatened. You need me."

"Okay," she said, surprised at how relieved she felt at his offer. She might not trust him completely, but as far as she knew he was on her side. "I've got a Metro pass. We can take the subway to the main train station and be in Venice later tonight."

"I'll need to grab a few things from my hotel on the way," he said, "but that won't take long."

She nodded, the lingering anxiety still twisting in her gut.

She filled up the rest of the backpack with a couple of changes of clothes. They could be in Venice in a few hours, then all she had to do was find the artwork, and all of this would be over.

FOUR

Joe checked his phone again as Talia grabbed clothes out of a dresser drawer, wondering if he'd just made the right decision. No messages. He probably should have insisted she stay and let him head to Venice and see if he could find the paintings on his own. He could easily call in for backup from either the FBI or someone from the local law enforcement right here in Rome. Someone who could stay with her and ensure her safety somewhere off the grid, where she couldn't be found.

But there were two things that stopped him from making that suggestion. One, she knew far better than he did where to look for the paintings, which meant they would probably find them much faster together than if he was searching on his own. And with the clock ticking in this situation, he didn't have the luxury of time on his side. And two, going together to Venice meant he'd be able to keep an eye on her himself. Besides, from what he'd learned about her from their brief time together, he had a feeling she never would have agreed to stay put here in Rome and do nothing.

Which meant all he could do was pray he'd made the right decision. He glanced at her as she dropped her passport into her bag and caught the determined set of her chin. He was right about one thing—she wouldn't have stayed here in Rome no matter how he tried to convince her. This situation might be personal for him, but it was personal to her, as well. And the bottom line was he'd rather be the one looking out for her than someone he didn't know.

"Any messages yet?" She swung her backpack over her shoulder and let out a deep breath.

"Nothing yet," he said. "But we'll hear from them soon. I promise."

"Okay. Then I think I'm ready."

He hesitated in the doorway and caught her gaze. "We're going to find those paintings, Talia, along with whoever's behind this."

"I hope so."

They headed out of her apartment and down the narrow staircase leading back down to the first floor of her building. He'd caught the worry along with doubt in her voice, and understood that feeling. He knew what it was like to lose a sibling, and he was going to do everything in his power to keep both her and her sister safe.

Which he would. The Dallas police department would watch out for Shelby, and he'd keep track of Talia. Because seriously, how much trouble could she get into riding the train north to the century-old city? They'd arrive in Venice, make contact with her brother-in-law, then search for the paintings. And if all went well, they'd find what they were looking for.

He had local Italian law enforcement looking for the man who'd broken into her apartment. Once they found and interrogated him, they'd find out who was behind this. And he'd be able to close the case. Simple. And once they discovered all the players in this, he'd have the answers he needed to know who'd murdered his brother.

As long as they did it all within seventy-two hours. He glanced at Talia. The problem was no case involving money, greed and murder was ever simple. And whoever was behind this had already killed at least once. Which only raised the stakes.

Once they reached the bottom of the staircase, Joe opened the door and stepped back out on the noisy street and bright sunlight. A rush of hot, humid air surrounded him.

He stopped on the sidewalk as the door clicked shut behind them and he scanned the busy street for signs of the man who'd broken in to Talia's apartment. No one looked familiar, but he could be anywhere. Watching them from inside one of the other buildings or from the rooftop. Which was why for the moment he was going to focus on getting her safely to Venice and count on the local police to track down their assailant.

"This way," he said, turning left at the light.

Talia paused on the sidewalk. "The subway's straight ahead."

"I know, but I think it's safer to go the long way in case we have a tail." Joe grabbed her hand and picked up his pace. If someone was following them, he planned to lose them before they ever hit the transit system. "It's just a precaution."

But while he didn't want her to worry, he certainly felt on edge. He searched the crowded streets, looking for anyone that seemed familiar or was acting suspicious. He felt her fingers clench tighter around his, escalating his need to protect her. He knew what it was like to lose someone close to you. And he didn't want it to happen to her again.

There was no sign of anyone following them as he led them down a narrow cobblestone lane, but he wasn't willing to take any chances. Because what he did know is that someone was out there, watching, and at this point he had no idea who it was.

"You okay?" he asked.

"Yeah. Just scared."

There was fear in her eyes when she glanced up at him. Her vulnerability tugged at him, but he wasn't going there. Not this time. She was vulnerable, but he had no intention of taking advantage. He was an agent and this was a case. Nothing more.

"It's like a game of cat and mouse," she said, barely above a whisper as they continued walking.

"The subways should be just a couple blocks back. If whoever is after the paintings is watching, it's more than likely they are going to assume we're headed to the main train station. But there's no reason to make this easy on them."

Five minutes later, he could see the sign again for the public transport. Talia was still looking behind them as they walked, clearly afraid that the man who'd broken in to her apartment was on their tail. He clutched her hand tighter.

She shivered next to him as they took the stairs down into the subway. "I can't shake the feeling someone's following us."

"Do you think you saw him?"

"I don't know. I keep thinking I do. Like I said, I might just be paranoid, but it makes sense they'd keep track of my every move if they think I have the paintings."

Joe glanced behind them as they went through the ticket barrier and punched their subway passes. He looked up at the ticker board as they walked onto the platform. There was two minutes until the next train appeared. It was crowded, which hopefully meant that if anyone had followed them, they wouldn't try anything, but that hadn't stopped their assailant from grabbing her bag at the Colosseum.

A group of Japanese tourists huddled near the edge of the platform. A woman pushed a stroller past them. A businessman talked on his phone.

"He's here." Talia grabbed his arm.

"Where?"

"A dozen yards or so behind us."

"Okay, I spotted him." Joe grabbed her hand. "Stay close to me, but keep an eye on him. Let's see if he follows us onto the train."

The platform was so congested they barely had enough space to move as the throng pressed toward the yellow line. The lights of the subway on the opposite side of the tracks shot through the darkness of the tunnel. Seconds later, the subway car rushed by, followed by the squealing of brakes as it came to a stop.

They still had another minute until their train arrived.

"He just slipped behind a pole," she said.

One second she was there beside him, the next second she was gone.

"Talia…" He scanned the platform for a glimpse of her pink shirt, but she'd already disappeared into the crowd.

Talia heard Joe calling her name, but she ignored his plea and instead pushed her way across the Metro platform toward where she'd last seen the man. Something inside her had snapped. He'd broken in to her apartment, and as much as she wanted to get away from him, she needed to put a stop to this. This man had threatened not just her, but her sister, as well. She couldn't erase the photos he'd sent her from her mind, either. The one of Thomas's body. The one of her and Joe sitting at the café. Someone was determined to get what they wanted, but she was just as determined to put a stop to all of this.

Except she'd lost him.

She searched the crowd, breathing in the smell of cigarette smoke and body odor brought on from the hot summer temperature. Graffiti blurred along the paint-chipped walls of the Metro. The train was coming into the station. Someone pushed past her, anxious for the doors to open and the exiting passengers to alight. But she kept moving through the crowd, her focus on the man with the streak of blond she'd just seen.

Two officers who stood talking on the other end of the platform caught her attention. She swallowed any doubts that what she was doing was foolish. She'd be safe. He wouldn't try anything here. Not with all of these people and security around them.

Her heart raced as she scanned the crowd. This wasn't exactly the way she'd planned on spending her afternoon. Having this man grab her bag, being rescued by the FBI, finding her apartment trashed and then having the intruder threatening her with a gun. Her gut churned as she pressed her bag closer to her side and glanced back at where she'd last seen Joe. But even he couldn't fix everything. She still couldn't get a hold of her sister, and there were no guarantees that going to Venice was going to put an end to this. Because if she couldn't find the paintings, nothing she did was going to matter.

Someone bumped into her from behind. While taking the Metro was the easiest way to travel, she always preferred avoiding rush hour, where it always seemed as if the entire city was riding the subway. Like right now.

She glanced around the platform, but there was no sign of the man. But he must have *her* in his sights. She had the same feeling of being watched as she'd felt earlier at the Colosseum.

She shifted her gaze to the left. Bingo. He was still there, lingering at the edge of the crowd. He hesitated briefly, then quickly turned around and headed for the exit. But he wasn't getting away. Not this time.

The crowd was thinning out around her as she started running. She grabbed his arm and pulled him around to face him. The familiar gaze pierced through hers. She swallowed the lump of fear in her throat, but didn't let go. She was right. It was him.

"Tell me who are you and who's after my sister," she said in Italian.

Talia caught the look of surprise in his eyes as he tried to pull away, but she just held on tighter. He'd threatened not just her, but Shelby, as well. This had to end.

"I said who are you?" she repeated when he didn't answer.

"You shouldn't have done this." He grabbed her arm and pressed a gun to her side. "You should have done what you were told, because now you've just made me mad and made this whole situation a whole lot worse."

"You can't shoot me here in front of all these people. There are cameras and police officers—"

"Except I don't have anything to lose." He leaned closer to her. "Which means I wouldn't test me if I were you."

There was anger in his voice, but she also caught the fear. What did he mean, he didn't have anything to lose?

"Who are you?"

"That doesn't matter."

"Then tell me who you're working with."

"A very bad person." He shook his head. "Do you think this is a game? Because it's not. I'm just a pawn, hired to ensure you do what you were told to do. The person who hired me…I meant what I said earlier. They've killed before and trust me, they will kill you—and your sister—if you don't do what they want."

Someone shouted *"Pistola!"*

Gun!

Talia turned around. A woman was screaming in Italian for the police. Taking advantage of the distraction, Talia pulled her arm away from the man and slipped through the crowd. But it was too late for him. The police had surrounded the man.

Crowds filled the platform and the scene was chaos. She never should have left Joe. She needed to find him. Needed to get out of here.

"Talia…" Someone grabbed her from behind—Joe. He whisked her back toward the platform. "What did you think you were doing?"

"I don't know. I saw him, and then…and then something snapped. I had to confront him." Her hands were shaking, her chest heaving. "What do we do now? They're going to be looking for me, and we don't have time to explain this to the police."

Another subway was pulling into the station.

"You're right. Let's go."

The doors of the newly arrived car whooshed

open, letting the dozens of riders escape, filling the platform even more. Joe kept walking, then pulled her into the subway car. The doors slid shut a fraction of a second later.

Talia glanced out the window from the safety of the Metro train. She couldn't see much, but it appeared that the police now had the man in their custody. Her legs shook as they found two empty seats in the back of the car.

"Talia…"

She looked up at him, unable to tell if he was furious with her, or simply relieved she was okay.

"That was stupid," she said. "I'm sorry. I never should have confronted him."

"Stupid, maybe, but on the other hand incredibly brave. But you could have been hurt."

"I know." She pressed the palms of her hands against her thighs to stop them from shaking. "But all I could think about was stopping him. To make this entire nightmare go away. I wanted to find out who he was, or who's behind this."

"Tell me what he said."

"He told me I should have done what I'd been told. That I'd made the entire situation worse." She drew in a deep breath. "But there was something else."

"What do you mean?"

"Something in his eyes. I don't know. He told me he didn't have anything to lose. He was scared, Joe. And I'm not sure why."

"He's being used by the person who killed your husband."

"I know. And now we've got the police involved. They're going to be looking for me now."

"I'll talk to my Italian contact. I already sent in a description of the man. I'll let him know that the police have him in custody and make sure someone questions him for answers regarding this case."

"And in the meantime?" she asked.

"I think we still need to head north and see if we can find those paintings. Because this is far from over."

FIVE

She was losing it. Talia felt the windows of the Metro close in on her as they sped into the darkness through tunnels that threatened to crush her. She tried to reassure herself that the car was filled with tourists carrying backpacks and businessmen reading newspapers. *Not* the man who'd broken in to her apartment. He'd been arrested by police and wasn't going anywhere for the moment. Which should make her feel better. But it didn't. At least not completely. Whoever wanted the paintings—whoever had killed her husband—was still out there. And after all that had happened in the past few hours, having their hired thug arrested and put behind bars wasn't going to stop them.

And that had her terrified.

She tried drawing in a calming breath as she counted down the subway stops to the hotel, where Joe needed to pick up his bag. She needed a place to clear her mind and stop shaking. Somewhere away from the stuffy Metro, full of people. The double doors finally opened at their stop, spewing out a dozen passengers including her and Joe, while more people filled the open space they'd left behind.

She felt Joe's hand on her elbow as they walked down the crowded platform and up the steep flight of stairs to the street in silence. She knew if she started talking she was going to start crying and probably not be able to stop. And she didn't want to do that. What she wanted was a place where she could feel safe.

And that place wasn't here.

"Talia…" He squeezed harder on her elbow, causing her to flinch. "Are you okay?"

She jerked away, surprised at her response. How did she explain that she was scared stiff? That no matter how hard she tried to fight the panic that had welled up within her, it wouldn't go away? And that she had no idea how to shake it?

Instead of answering, she took him down a side street, to a quiet spot she knew was located off the beaten path, and slipped under a darkened archway. She'd always been drawn to the places off the main thoroughfares, where you'd never find tourists and their cameras. Her father had first showed her a number of Rome's hidden jewels, and those excursions had given her a zeal for the city that went far deeper than simply a shopping list of famous attractions.

She slowed down once they were inside the private courtyard and took in the familiar old buildings, with their twisted grapevines climbing up the sides, earth-colored paint jobs and flower-lined balconies. A woman glanced down from a third-story window and smiled before turning back to her laundry hanging in the wind above them. It was a quiet place, a reminder of what Rome had looked like decades ago. Simple. Unencumbered. And how her heart had once been before it had lost so much.

She turned around to face Joe, then held up her palm to stop him from talking. Not yet. She needed her heart to stop racing. She didn't need him feeling sorry for her. She just wanted to find a way to put an end to this before someone else got hurt.

"I'm sorry." She drew in a deep breath, let it out slowly then sat down on a cracked step leading up to one of the apartments. "I just need a quiet place to calm my nerves for a few minutes."

The sun shone on him as he looked down at her, bringing out red and blond highlights in his hair. "You have nothing to be sorry for."

She swallowed hard. "That's easy for you to say. You're an FBI agent. You know how to handle situations like this, but I don't. I'm used to spending my days showing tourists this city, but this... I don't know how to deal with people threatening my life and the lives of my family."

"Which is why I'm coming with you. So you don't have to deal with this on your own."

"And if that's not enough?" She heard her voice rising and pressed her lips together in an attempt to stop her emotions from spiraling out of control. He didn't deserve her backlash. "The point is that you can't guarantee my protection. Or my sister's. We don't know who's behind this, but we do know how far they are willing to go. They've already murdered at least one person."

He sat down beside her. "Take a deep breath."

Talia frowned. She didn't want to take a deep breath. She wanted to run away as far as she could and forget any of this happened. She wanted to go back to a time when all she had to worry about was the occasional obnoxious tourist. Not this.

Besides, she'd come to Italy to get away from losing Thomas, and now it was as if it was starting all over again. She didn't want to deal with her past. Didn't want to relive to the moment when her heart had been broken by all the lies he'd told her.

She looked at Joe, who was sitting just close enough to where their shoulders were touching on the narrow staircase. She really didn't know anything about him. Only that he'd agreed to come with her, and that her heart kept telling her to trust him. But was his presence going to be enough to keep her safe? Thomas had been a cop, and it hadn't saved him. Nor had it stopped him from betraying her.

But Joe wasn't Thomas. And it wasn't fair for her to make that comparison.

"I just feel as if it's happening all over again," she said, breaking the silence between them. "The days after Thomas's death were like a nightmare. Not only did I have to deal with questions from our friends about what had happened, but the police believed that I knew about what he had been doing. That I had somehow been in on it. After he was killed they brought me in to an interrogation room, read me my rights and made me sit for hours of questioning."

"I can't imagine how difficult that must have been."

No matter how hard she tried, she couldn't stop the flow of memories from seeping through the cracked walls she'd diligently placed around herself. "How do you explain to your close friends, to his parents, that the man you'd fallen in love with and married—the man you'd trusted with your life—had been leading a double life? Once the police were finally convinced I wasn't involved, I decided to move here. I was so tired of the questions and people avoiding me because they didn't know what to say. Especially when all I needed was for them to ask me how I was doing, and did I need someone to talk to?"

"Tell me about this place," he said. "I'm assuming it's not just a random courtyard you stumbled into."

He was trying to distract her. Giving her the time she needed to take back control of her emotions, despite the wave of reminders that refused to let up.

"My father loved history. He brought us to Italy almost every summer while we were growing up. He came specifically to teach at one of the local universities, but during his time off we explored the city and countryside. And while at some point we hit all the famous tourist attractions, he and my mother always preferred discovering the places most visitors had never even heard of. The places where only the locals went."

"Like this little corner of the city."

She nodded. "We'd head off on Saturdays and Sunday afternoons and comb through cemeteries, and rose gardens, and churches. Then we'd head off to one of his favorite cafés and eat homemade pasta or dumplings. My father always complained about it not being quite as good as his Italian grandmother's, but he always ended up ordering seconds and eating every bite."

She smiled at the memory, knowing things couldn't have stayed the same, but how she'd do anything for one more meal sitting across the table from her father with the scent of fresh basil and mozzarella between them as they talked about history and politics.

"And Thomas? Where did you meet him?"

She hesitated at the question.

"Thomas was the son of a colleague of my father's. We were introduced one summer. I was smitten from day one. Thomas was four years older, so it took a bit longer for him, but he seemed…perfect. He was Italian, good-looking, and my father approved, which was important to me."

"And your parents now? Have they been supportive?"

"They died in a car wreck before Thomas was killed. They never knew what he'd done. It would have crushed them. Just like it's crushed his parents. None of us ever guessed what he'd been involved in. I still find it hard to believe."

Joe's phone ran, pulling her back into the present.

"Give me a second. It's Esposito, my contact with the Italian crime team."

She watched Joe stand up and step away as he listened to his contact on the other end of the line. A minute later he hung up and turned back to her.

"He was able to get some information on the man the police arrested at the Metro."

"Who is he?"

"His name is Matteo Arena. He hasn't said much so far, but it sounds like you were right about him being scared. The officers interrogating him believe someone has been holding something over him."

"Blackmail."

Joe nodded.

"What else has he told the police?"

"Not much. He seems to be more scared of whoever hired him than the police. He hasn't given them any names. But with us not there to press charges, there's a good chance they'll let him go eventually unless they can find some more evidence."

"But we need to keep going," she said. Her heart had finally slowed down, but that didn't mean the fear had completely vanished.

"You don't have to come to Venice with me. I can do it on my own."

She shook her head. "I want to come. I need to. Sitting here twiddling my thumbs will only drive me crazy."

"Okay." He shoved his phone into his back pocket and hesitated. "I know we haven't known each other long, but you can trust me."

"I'm trying."

"I know."

She let him help her up off the stair, then quickly pulled her hand away as she took one last look at the peaceful courtyard. "Let's go."

Fifteen minutes later, Joe stepped into the kind of cookie-cutter hotel room that could be found in any major city around the world. Its basic amenities consisted of a flat-screen TV, abstract art on the wall and a view of the parking lot. But he'd picked the chain for its location, not for its Italian charm. He pulled his backpack out of the hotel closet and dumped in enough clothes for the next couple of days, then stuck his wallet and passport inside a zippered pouch to hopefully deter pickpockets.

He glanced at Talia, who stood at the long window looking out over a row of cars By the time they'd made it back onto the Metro, she'd seemed calmer. And instead of panic, that inner strength he'd first noticed—despite everything that had happened to her—had begun to emerge.

Vulnerable yet capable. Broken yet still strong.

There were still so many things he didn't know about her. What triggered her panic? What calmed her down? He dropped in his shaving kit then zipped up his bag and dropped it onto the bed, wishing none of those questions mattered to him. But for some reason they did. She'd already dealt with losing her husband, and while her wounds seemed to be mostly healed, having to rehash the investigation and Thomas's ultimate betrayal all over again couldn't be easy.

Still, he had to fight the feelings of familiarity. The feeling that he'd known her for years rather than just a few hours. Because he didn't know her. Not really. He might have become good at reading people, but he'd barely scratched the surface of who she really was. And yet somehow, he couldn't suppress his feelings of wanting to learn more about her.

The problem was that as soon as this was over he was going to leave for Washington and she was going to stay here. Which was why any connection he might feel toward her didn't matter. He'd do everything he could to protect her, but that didn't mean falling for her. And even though he might understand what it meant to lose someone, he wasn't going to let her vulnerability wedge a hole in his heart.

He'd done that once before. Allowed his heart to get involved when he should have left well enough alone. That was the only way this job worked. Treating every case for what it was, a file with a number that needed to be solved. Because that's what they were.

That's all Talia ever could be to him.

"Better?" he asked, grabbing his charging cell phone off the table.

She turned around and looked at him. "For the moment. I'm sorry I fell apart."

"I've already said you have nothing to be sorry about. You've been through a lot today, and unfortunately we both know it's not over."

She shook her head and turned back to the window. "I've always been the strong one in the family. Especially after my parents died. My sister was always reminding me that I was the glue holding both of us together, but today... I don't know. Maybe it's all the memories of the past surfacing at the same time... but I feel anything but strong."

"Having to hold your family together isn't easy." He knew, because he'd tried that for years, as well.

"No, it's not."

"We'll figure this out, Talia. I promise."

She nodded and picked up her bag. "I know. I just hope that in the meantime no one else gets caught in the crossfire."

He caught the pain in her eyes as she blinked back the tears. He knew what she was thinking. It wasn't just her life that was hanging in the balance, it was her sister's, as well. Which was why this case was different.

Talia wasn't just a number.

And this time he wasn't just trying stop the

looting of rare artifacts from museums or catch
a dealer trafficking art by making undercover
deals in some shady hotel room. It was personal. He needed to ensure her safety from
whoever had killed her husband. And make
sure someone else didn't die because of them.

"You ready?" she asked, breaking into his
thoughts.

He nodded, took one more look around the
room, then shoved the hotel card key into his
pocket and slipped into the hallway behind her.

Rome's central train station was more like
an airport terminal with its clusters of shops
and restaurants, long lines of travelers pulling
suitcases and dozens of ticket machines. An
announcement was being made over the loud-
speaker in Italian as he finished buying two
tickets to Venice via Florence from one of the
self-service machines.

"Train's leaving on time," Talia said, repo-
sitioning her backpack on her shoulder as they
merged back into the throng of travelers.

"Good." Joe glanced up at the large electronic departures board. "Which means we've
got about ten minutes to get to the platform."

So far, so good. He didn't think they were
being followed, but they clearly weren't out

of the woods yet. Not until he had the paintings in his hand and he could put an end to this. Which had him once again second-guessing his decision to bring her with him. The crowded terminal made it harder to protect her, which meant he was simply going to have to be even more diligent. He continued studying passengers as they made their way to the platform, because while the man in the hoodie might be in police custody, he wasn't the only one involved.

The train had just arrived when they reached platform six. They stepped up onto the train and headed down the narrow aisle and found their assigned seats. He nodded at her to take the window seat, then sat down beside her. Passengers were filing onto the train and stowing bags above them before sitting down in their seats.

"I was wondering if you had a file on the cases." Talia unscrewed the lid to the bottle of water she'd bought and took a long drink. "I'd like to know everything there is about both cases and how they connect."

Joe reached for his backpack then pulled out a folder from the back zippered section. "I thought you might. I was given permission for you to see this, but let me warn you that there are a lot of codes, file numbers and redacted text throughout the paperwork."

Talia took the folder, opened it and began scanning the first page.

She shook her head. "You're right. I might need you to translate most of this. What's CIPAV, for example?"

Joe smiled. "That stands for Computer and Internet Protocol Address Verifier. It's used to track and gather location data on suspects under electronic surveillance."

"Like Thomas?"

"Not in this instance. He wasn't on anyone's radar until the night he died." He glanced out the window as they pulled out of the station and the train began picking up speed. "But one of the suspects connected to the museum robbery was being watched by the FBI."

"So where do we start?" she asked.

"I'd like to go over the list of everyone who was in on the raid that day, as well as the dealers and gang members connected to the case, and compare them to the list of people who were at the museum that day. I'm convinced there's a connection."

"Didn't the police already do that?"

"Yes, but that doesn't mean something wasn't missed."

She dropped the folder onto her lap and glanced up at him. "Can I ask you something first?"

"Sure."

"Whenever you talk about this case— especially the museum robbery—your voice… I don't know, but it seems like this is more than just another case. Like it's personal to you."

Joe hesitated. Disconnecting his personal life from his work was usually easy. There were some divisions of the FBI where agents dealt with victims of violent crime and trauma on a regular basis. But for the most part, he spent his time investigating and recovering stolen pieces of art, and sorting mounds of paperwork. But she was right. This time there was no chance to escape the connection between the two cases. But he'd planned to avoid telling her about it. His jaw tensed. He'd convinced himself that there was no reason for her to know the truth behind his interest in the case. But if that was true, then why did he suddenly have the urge to tell her the entire story?

"Joe…what is it?"

He turned back to her and caught her gaze. "I told you about the man who was killed in a museum robbery? And how the bullet they found in the body matched the bullet that had killed your husband?"

"Yes."

He stared out the window as the train whizzed by acres of green fields and passed small towns surrounded by groves of trees. He'd been told by a colleague that the views of the Italian countryside from the train were stunning, but he didn't really see any of it. Instead, all he could see was a body with a bullet through the head, lying on a slab of concrete at the morgue.

Something that never should have happened.

"That man," he said, turning back to her. "That man was my brother."

SIX

"Your brother?" Talia caught the marked pain in Joe's eyes. "Wow. I had no idea. I'm so sorry."

"Me, too."

As surprised as she was with his revelation, the all-too-personal facts of the case suddenly lined up. "Which means the gun that fired the shot and killed my husband killed your brother. And it explains why this isn't just about finding some lost pieces of art."

"No." He looked at her, seeming to stare right through her. "I'm here because I want to find out who killed my brother, and make sure it doesn't happen again to someone else."

While she might be surprised at the connection between the two murders, from the moment they'd met outside the Colosseum she'd sensed an intensity toward his job. A purpose fueled by a hidden motivation. But this connection to the case and the death of his brother... She hadn't realized it was so personal. His brother's death explained that motivation. Explained his insistence on coming with her to Venice to find the paintings. He was determined to find whoever was behind this and hand them over to the authorities himself.

Two connected murders. One gun. No suspects. He wanted—needed—closure to the case. And she understood why. She needed the same thing, as well.

"Tell me about your brother," she said.

While she waited for him to respond, the train sped through a darkened tunnel, then emerged a few seconds later on the other side, back into the bright, morning sunshine.

Joe rubbed the back of his neck, seemingly in no hurry to answer. "Ryan had only been working at the museum a couple months as a security guard. Ironically, I was the one who got him the job."

"It's interesting how you both worked jobs connected to the art world."

"While my dad couldn't draw a stick figure if his life depended on it, our mom was an artist. I have an appreciation for art, Ryan had her gift and planned to use his working in film.

Animation in particular. I read it in your file that you're an artist, too."

She fiddled with the cap of her water bottle, noticing his change in subject. "Seems like a lifetime ago since I actually finished a project. Before moving to Rome I studied art in Florence and later at a couple universities in the States. I eventually started teaching. And while I loved instructing, I ended up not having enough time to do my own work. I was actually looking to make some changes career-wise, but then Thomas died, and I moved here instead."

"I'd love to see some of your artwork."

She shook her head. "Like I said, I haven't painted for a long time."

Not since Thomas had died.

The counselor she'd gone to a couple times had told her it would be therapeutic for her to keep painting, but for some reason she'd lost her joy in the process, and had yet to rediscover it.

"Tell me more about your brother and the day he died," she said, turning the conversation back to him.

Joe shifted in his seat next to her, the pain of his brother's death clearly still raw. "He was twenty-two years old. He planned on marrying his girlfriend, then settling down and working toward his postgraduate degree."

"It's frightening how quickly your world can turn upside down. Thomas's death...your brother's death. Both completely unanticipated."

"It was all over the news at the time. Two men, looking like tourists, walked into the museum in the middle of the day, grabbed a painting off the wall worth half a million dollars and started walking out, just like they'd done the past two robberies they were involved in."

"That's a pretty brazen way to rob a museum."

"Exactly. And hard to believe they've gotten away with it so many times."

"And your brother? How was he involved?"

"We've been able to put together a rough timeline. Apparently Ryan was doing his rounds and noticed that the painting was gone. He called his boss to verify if the painting was being cleaned, because it wasn't on the list. When the curator said no, he headed for the museum entrance. According to video surveillance, he missed the thieves taking the piece by a matter of seconds. Which was why he managed to catch up with them as they were getting ready to walk out the front door. When he tried to detain them, one of them panicked and shot him, then they both ran out of the museum and disappeared."

There was something comforting about talking to him, not as an FBI agent, but simply as someone who had lost someone he'd cared about. It brought them to the same level and allowed her to understand him better.

"Were you able to identify them?" she asked. "There has to be some evidence of who they were."

"We have video from all the robberies, but the men had clearly staked out the museum before they hit. They managed to avoid the camera in all three situations. The only other evidence is a set of fingerprints one of them left on a broken frame, but he was never identified." Joe's jaw tensed. "The only thing we do have is a description from Ryan."

"So you were able to speak with him before he died?"

"One of the officers at the scene did. By the time I got to him, he'd already been rushed to the hospital. He died on the operating table, before I had a chance to see him."

"I know how hard that had to have been."

When Thomas had been shot, her greatest regret had been that she hadn't been able to talk with him before he died. She remembered the morning he'd left for work like it was yesterday. They'd fought about something stupid. She'd accused him of never cleaning up his morning coffee mess.

And those were the last words she'd spoken to him.

No goodbyes. No "I'm sorry." Just a casket and a funeral to plan, along with the police's accusations that he'd been a dirty cop.

Joe leaned back in his seat and caught her gaze. "What makes me angry is that his death never should have happened. A two-hundred-year-old painting isn't worth his life. It's not worth anyone's life. But instead I received a phone call telling me to go immediately to the hospital."

All in an instant, just like her situation. Everything changed.

She'd received her own phone calls. First when her parents had died. Later about Thomas. Both came with an initial shock. That feeling that you were going to wake up soon, but you never did. And Thomas's betrayal had been an added thorn that had wedged its way through her heart.

"I know I'm not the only one who's lost someone," he said, catching her gaze.

"It is hard," she said. "That initial shock and the numbness at first. Then everything begins to wear off and all you want to do is escape from the emotions."

She took another sip of her water, surprised at how easy it was to talk with him. Maybe it was because with his own loss, he understood to an extent what she had gone through.

"Did they ever find the gun used to kill your brother?" she asked.

"It was found in a Dumpster a half a mile from the museum. As far as we can tell, they escaped on foot at least that far."

"The same gun that killed Thomas."

Joe nodded.

"You can't assume that there's a connection to Thomas's case, though," she continued. "What I mean is just because the same weapon was used, doesn't mean that the cases are related."

"That is true, but there were a number of other things we've discovered that tied the two cases."

"For instance?"

"The robbery that killed my brother was one of several over a time period of about five years where high-priced, easy-to-carry-out items were stolen. We have evidence that all of the robberies are connected and that the perpetrators have links to a local drug cartel. And the three Li Fonti paintings we're looking for were taken from the second museum robbery."

She glanced down the narrow aisle of the train. A couple people were reading books. A businessman worked on his computer. A young mother was trying to keep her toddler occupied. She worked to keep her thoughts focused. Joe's conclusions made sense. But it also meant that Thomas had managed to cross some dangerous people. And in the end it had gotten him killed.

She turned back to Joe. "Thank you."

"For what?"

"For coming with me. You could have pulled the 'I'm an agent' card and made me stay in Rome with some of your babysitters. And I know this is personal for you, but even after all these years, I need answers, as well."

"And that's what we're going to get."

Her phone rang and she checked the ID. It was her sister. She quickly answered the call. "Shelby? Are you okay?"

"Okay? No, I'm not okay. Not at all. What in the world is going on?" She sounded frantic. Hysterical. "I was just pulled out of class by my principal and now some FBI agents want me to leave and go to some safe house. I had to beg them to let me use my phone to call you."

"What did they tell you?"

"Not much. That some lunatic is stalking me, and they have photos to prove it, *and* then they told me that this is somehow all connected to Thomas and some drug cartel."

"Shelby—"

"But that makes no sense," her sister continued, not letting Talia get a word in edgewise. "Thomas is dead. How can all of this have to do with him? And the cartel? Seriously?"

"Shelby, stop. Take a deep breath and listen to me." Talia let out a sharp breath of her own, then sent Joe an apologetic look. Her sister had always been the dramatic one. And this situation was clearly not going to be an exception.

"Fine. Just tell me what's going on," Shelby said.

"I'm still trying to figure out everything as well, but there are a set of valuable paintings someone is after. They believe Thomas stole them, and that I now have them. They're using you as leverage to get me to turn them over."

"You can't be serious. There are people threatening to kill me? This sounds more like some Jason Bourne movie. Not my life. Remember, I spend my days teaching kindergartners to read, to count objects and classify options. Not evade hit men and the cartel."

"It's not going to come to that. The FBI will keep you safe. You don't have to worry."

"Right. Do you have them? These paintings?"

"No." Talia hesitated. "Well...maybe."

"I don't understand."

"It's likely that they were in some of Thomas's things. We're on our way to Venice now to track them down. His mother remembers seeing them."

"Wait a minute...who is *we*?"

"I'm traveling with an FBI agent."

"An FBI agent." Shelby let out a high-pitched laugh. "Of course you are, because there's nothing strange at all about your traveling across Italy with an FBI agent while trying to track down some stolen paintings. And by the way, how much are these paintings worth?"

Talia hesitated before giving her sister an answer. "Depending on the buyer, he told me about half a million—"

"Are you serious?"

"Each."

"Well, no wonder they want them back."

"Shelby, listen. Just do what they tell you to

do. They'll take you somewhere safe for the next couple of days. This will all be over soon."

"I can't just leave my job—"

"It's going to be okay. I promise." Talia hung up the phone a minute later, then dropped it into her lap, wondering if she should have made a promise she wasn't sure she could keep. "That, as I'm sure you could guess, was my sister."

"That didn't sound like it went too well."

"She's upset, but I can't say that I blame her. They're taking her somewhere safe for a few days until this blows over." Her fingers gripped the armrest. "But at least she's okay."

Joe leaned forward, wishing things could be different for both of them. He wished his brother was still alive, that Talia hadn't have gone through the loss she had. But what was it that the Bible said? God causes the sun to rise on both the evil and the good, and the rain to fall on both the righteous and the unrighteous. There was no way of avoiding the difficulties.

But he could do everything in his power to get her through this one unharmed.

"I meant what I said. I'm going to do everything I can to make sure that both you and your sister are okay."

"Except neither of us can guarantee the outcome. I shouldn't have made the promise to my sister, and you can't make me that promise. Life doesn't exactly turn out the way you'd like it to sometimes."

A woman sat down a few rows ahead of them, pulling his attention momentarily away from their conversation. He couldn't pinpoint what it was, but there was something familiar about her.

"Joe, what is it?"

The fear was back in her eyes. He knew she wanted to think that they were safe now. That there wasn't anyone out there—or on this train for that matter—who could touch them. That they'd simply arrive in Venice, find the paintings and put an end to all of this.

But he knew it might not be that easy.

"I guess this time you're not the only one who's paranoid."

"You think we're being watched?"

"Maybe. I'm not sure."

Joe studied the passengers in the car they were in. "There's a woman four rows in front of us, thirtysomething and wearing a purple shirt and jeans and facing us. I can't figure out what it is, but I think I've seen her before."

"Where?" she asked.

"I don't know…maybe from the Colosseum. Maybe on the street sometime this afternoon."

He watched as the woman grabbed a book from her bag and started reading. He couldn't figure out exactly what it was, but the feeling kept nagging at him. Matteo Arena had managed to follow them through the subway station and he'd been arrested, but they knew there was someone else behind all of this. Someone with enough skin in the game to ensure they knew exactly where they were at all times. Someone who could be there when they found the paintings and see that Talia didn't hand them over to the FBI.

He shifted his gaze out the window again. Acres of vineyards stretched endlessly beyond the tracks. But maybe like Talia he was just being paranoid. He'd always tried to stay focused with his cases. Impartial and detached, in order to make sure he didn't miss something. But as unsettled as he was feeling at the moment, he was trained to be observant and he knew he'd seen her before.

He turned back to Talia. "Let's go over this again. What exactly happened between you and the intruder in your apartment before I arrived?"

She hesitated briefly, pressing her lips together. "He—he pulled out a gun and told me I should have shown up with the paintings."

"And after that?" Joe persisted.

"He told me to give him my bag."

"Okay. And did you?"

"I tossed it to him, and he then proceeded to empty everything onto my bed like he didn't believe me." Her brow furrowed as she looked across at him. "What are you thinking?"

He glanced down at the floor beside her. "That's the same bag he went through?"

"Yeah, he didn't take it. I just dumped everything that I needed back into it before we left."

He jutted his chin at the bag. "Do you mind?"

"No. Of course not." She quickly handed it to him. "But what are you looking for?"

"A tracking device."

He caught her surprised expression as he began meticulously going through the contents of the bag near the window, making sure he was out of the line of sight of the woman and any other passengers. He glanced at Talia, hoping she really didn't mind him invading her space. But if he was right, they needed to know. He pulled out a makeup bag, lotion, hand sanitizer and her passport among a number of miscellaneous things, and stopped himself from smiling. He'd never been able to figure out how a woman could pack so much stuff in such a small space.

"Any pockets?" he asked, running his hand down the sides.

"There's a zippered one."

He found the closed pouch, unzipped it, then reached inside. He pulled out the small GPS no bigger than a dime and set it on his thigh.

Talia leaned forward. "You've got to be kidding me. He bugged me?"

"It looks like it, and it explains a lot. He must have slipped it into your bag at the apartment when he searched it. Which meant he was able to follow us into the subway and didn't have to worry about losing us."

"What about the woman?" she asked, glancing at the figure who was still reading. "Do you really think she's in on this?"

"I don't know." He looked again at the woman who was still reading. She still hadn't turned a page. He pulled out a tissue from Talia's purse before putting everything back inside. "But we know he wasn't working alone. Someone's behind this. Someone who wants to make sure they get what they are after."

"Give me a second," he said. "I want you to stay here."

He dropped the GPS into his pocket, then stood up and headed down the aisle. He snapped a couple of photos of the woman with his phone while pretending to text. Not that anyone noticed. Most of the passengers had earphones in as they listened to music or were fiddling with their phones. They certainly weren't paying attention to anything going on around them. And neither, it seemed, was she.

He walked up to the suspicious woman, dropped the tissue on the floor, then bent down to pick it up, quickly sizing her up. He'd bet his bank account that she was an American, primarily due to the North Face backpack beside her, and the book she was reading.

He caught her gaze and nodded as he picked up the tissue and knocked over her bag with his foot. "Sorry."

She leaned forward to set her bag upright and nodded. The amber pendent of her necklace caught the light.

He stood up and kept walking, certain now. He remembered now where he'd seen her. The woman had been sitting across the narrow street from them, at an outside table in front of the café, looking like a tourist, when he and Talia had first sat down. When Talia had received another text message.

And what were the chances that the same woman was now on her way north on the same train. Another coincidence?

He didn't think so.

The train took a curve, throwing him slightly off balance. He gripped the back of a seat and caught himself before going on. He watched her through the reflection of the window as she slipped her book into her bag and started after him, further proving his theory that she was involved.

He stepped into the next car and kept walking, then quickly turned around and faced her.

"Excuse me," he began. "I'm sorry, it's just that you look familiar. Have we met?"

"I don't believe so." She spoke with a horrible Italian accent. "You must be mistaken."

"I don't think so. Perhaps at a party?" He was winging it, but he needed answers. And besides, what did he have to lose?

"I don't think so," she said, ignoring him.

"Actually it doesn't matter." He pulled out his badge and held it up. "I'm Agent Joe Bryant with the FBI. We need to talk."

He watched her face go pale. The Italian government knew he was here and while he didn't have the authority to make an arrest, she didn't have to know that.

"Like I said, you must be mistaken."

She darted under his arm and past him. He hesitated before following her, wondering where she thought she was going.

He followed her into the connecting car, as the train began to suddenly slow down, brakes squealing as it turned another corner.

"You've got to be kidding me."

"Joe?"

He glanced behind him. Talia stood behind him, carrying their backpacks. "I told you to stay in your seat."

"I didn't want to leave our bags, but I panicked when I saw you leave our train car. Did she say anything?"

"No, but her expression did when I told her I was FBI. And I think she just stopped the train."

Glass doors opened ahead of them. She hadn't just stopped the train, she was getting off.

He could see the lights of the next station ahead as the train slowed to a stop. He hesitated before jumping off the train to follow her.

"Joe..."

He could still see the woman as she ran

alongside the tracks. How was he supposed to protect Talia and go after their suspect at the same time? But he needed to know who this person was.

"Stay on the train, Talia."

He started running after the woman. Seconds later, two officers wearing polo shirts came around the bend, their weapons pointed at him. He stopped, then glanced behind him to where Talia stood out of breath, her eyes wide in horror.

"Talia…"

"The two of you need to come with us now."

SEVEN

"I've told you everything I know." Talia squeezed her hands in her lap until her nails bit into her palms. How had a simple train ride north turned into such a nightmare? "There was a woman on the train that looked familiar. I'd been followed earlier today. My apartment broken into. We thought she might somehow be involved. We just wanted to speak with her."

"What happened next?" The officer who had been questioning her for the past twenty minutes sat back in his chair and spoke to her in Italian, his gaze unwavering.

"I don't know." She slid to the edge of her seat and tapped her feet against the ground. "Agent Bryant left to ask her some questions. I came behind him a minute later. Then she pushed the emergency button to stop the train."

"And when the train stopped?"

"She got off."

She glanced up at the clock hanging on the wall. Every minute here meant another minute they weren't looking for the paintings.

A second man opened the door and signaled her interrogator to step out of the room.

The following minute alone was almost as bad as the barrage of questions. All she could hear was the ticking of the clock. Her feet tapped against the tiled floor. She had no idea where Joe was or what they were asking him.

I need some wisdom, God.

She needed for them to let her go.

This time both of the men stepped into the room.

She dropped her hands to her sides and stood up. "Can I go now? Please."

"Not yet." He nodded at the first man. "We have a few more questions we need to ask you. It's regarding the murder of your husband."

Talia felt as if the wind had been knocked out of her. As if she'd just fallen into some dark, tunnel in Alice's Wonderland and there was no way out.

"Wait a minute," she said. "My husband? I don't understand what he has to do with any of this."

"Please. Just sit down."

Talia sat back down on the cold metal chair

and felt the walls of the interrogation room close in around her. Her heart pounded inside her chest. Her hands felt sweaty. How had a this turned into an interrogation about Thomas? She let out a sharp breath. She'd been here before. It might be a different country and a different city, but it felt like the exact same room. The same looks shot at her by the uniformed men sitting on the other side of the table, staring at her as if she was guilty.

The questions had come in a steady stream the night Thomas died. *Had you and your husband been having problems in your marriage? What was your financial situation? Did you know anything about the extra money they'd found in a wired account?*

She'd sat there answering question after question for what seemed like hours. It wasn't until later that she'd found out that Thomas had been stealing from drug raids and other confiscated property. He was dead and unable to defend himself, but that hadn't stopped them from figuring out what he'd done.

At first, though, she hadn't believed them. She'd tried to convince them that Thomas would never have done something like that. But they'd quickly told her that all wives believed their husbands were innocent and implied she'd simply been too blind to see the truth.

Over the days and weeks that had followed, the reality of what he'd done finally began to sink in. How could she not have seen that something was wrong? Not to have known who he really was? His actions had left her shattered.

And now it was happening again.

"What does my husband's murder have to do with what happened today? He's been dead for three years."

"We had a tip—"

"Wait a minute...what kind of tip?"

The older of the two officers leaned forward and spoke to her in Italian. "We understand that your husband was accused of stealing, including some valuable paintings."

"How do you know that?"

"We will ask the questions. Is that true?"

Talia blinked back the tears. "Yes."

"So here's what I think might have happened. Your husband stole the money and paintings, but was unfortunately killed. But that didn't stop you from holding on to what you had until you could dispose of the items for a profit."

She ran her palm across her forehead as they

kept asking question after question. It was so hot in the room. Stifling hot. These were the same accusations she'd already heard. She glanced up at the second hand still ticking in the corner of the room. Some of the paint had chipped away along the edges of the ceiling. It didn't matter what she said. They didn't believe her.

"That case has been closed for years," she said. "My husband was found guilty, and I accept that, but I had nothing to with his death or the things that he stole. Just like I had nothing to do with stopping the train."

She reached for the bottle of water sitting in the middle of the table. Her head was swimming both from fatigue and fear.

The older man took a call, then stood up and nodded at her. "You're free to leave. For now."

She hesitated, wanting more information, but she clearly wasn't going to get it. Instead, she stepped out of the room. Joe was standing at the end of the hallway.

He started toward her. "Are you okay?"

"Not really." Her hands and legs were shaking. She felt weak and unsettled. And she just wanted to wake up from the nightmare.

"What did they want to know?" he asked.

"Questions about what we were doing on that train...and Thomas."

"Thomas?" Joe squeezed her shoulder before pulling his hand away. "I don't understand. Why would they bring his case up?"

"I asked them the same thing. They wouldn't give me a name, but someone called in a tip of some kind. But…" She fought back the emotions, trying not to cry. "It was like—it was like I was there again. The night Thomas died. The same questions and accusations about my involvement."

"I'm wondering if whoever's behind this has decided they don't want you getting to Venice."

"What do you mean?"

"It's the only thing that makes sense." He looked past her, as if he was trying to put the pieces together. "Think about it. Someone calls in an anonymous tip. Brings up questions about a murder you were once tied to—"

"And we get stuck defending ourselves to the police." The theory sent chills shooting up her spine. "But why? Do you think they just want us out of the picture now?"

"Maybe. If they know we're heading to Venice, they've probably also figured out you have family there. And maybe they've concluded that you know the paintings are there."

"And if they get there first, they don't have

to risk my keeping them for myself or turning them over to the FBI."

"We need to get to Venice," he said, turning back to her.

"It's too late now. The last train has already left, which means we can't get there 'til tomorrow."

She looked up at him and drew in a deep breath of frustration, unable to stop the surge of emotions. Exhaustion mingled with panic, making it hard for her to think clearly. They needed to put an end to this, but at this point, she didn't even know how.

She felt her eyes brim with tears. She started to turn away, but Joe pulled her toward him and wrapped his arms around her.

"I'm sorry," he said. "For all of this. But we're going to figure a way out."

She gave in and melted against his chest. She could feel her heart pounding against his. Smell the faint scent of his citrusy cologne. She pushed aside the unwanted feelings of attraction. That was a place she wasn't going.

Her phone rang, and she took a step back—both from Joe and her conflicted emotions—and answered the phone. It was Thomas's brother. She'd called him when they'd left

Rome to tell him they were on their way, then forgotten to tell him they'd been delayed.

"Marco?"

"I was just calling to see what time your train was coming in. I thought you'd already be here by now."

She wiped her cheek with the back of her hand. "We had a bit of a holdup, but we'll be on the first train out of Florence in the morning, which should put us in Venice around ten thirty."

"No problem. I'm heading out on the boat with Celso and a couple other friends for a late dinner, and didn't want to miss you. Just call me when you get in tomorrow. I'll be working, but should be able to stop by and let you into the house."

"I appreciate it."

She hesitated, wondering if she should say more. But she didn't want to tell him what was going on. Didn't want to take any chances of putting his life in danger. The less he knew, the better.

"Is everything okay?" he said. "You sound… I don't know. Upset."

"I'm fine. I'll explain everything when I get there."

Talia hung up the phone, then stared at the

cold, white tile of the police station as she walked outside beside Joe. They were stuck in Florence until morning and there was nothing she could do about it for now.

But what if tomorrow was too late?

Joe could see the fatigue in Talia's eyes as they walked out of the station. Darkness had long since fallen over the city, leaving its ancient landmarks aglow in yellow lights and leaving Talia looking over her shoulder.

He searched for what to say to her that would help. He could still smell the scent of vanilla from her hair when he'd stepped over the line and impulsively drawn her into his arms. But he knew how she felt. That fear she'd gone through in the hours and days after Thomas's death had only compounded with the feelings of betrayal.

"What do we do now?" she asked.

"I'll book a couple of rooms for us to stay in tonight. Then in the morning I'll talk with my contact in the Carabinieri, see if we can get some answers before we catch our train out of here."

It was what he did best. Whether it was his job or his personal life, he was used to making strategic plans, and then carrying them out.

He glanced at her in the glow of the streetlight and caught the faraway look in her eyes. The tense set of her jaw. Except there were some things he didn't know how to fix.

They kept walking side by side down the cobblestone sidewalk in silence. A group of musicians played music in a large square that was edged with restaurants and cafés. Even after dark, it was still busy with tourists and locals sitting outside a handful of cafés drinking coffee and eating.

"Do you ever feel like no matter how hard you try, you can't shake the past's hold?" she asked, breaking the silence between them.

"Yeah, actually. I have."

His thoughts jumped to Natasha. How often had her lies kept him from taking another chance at falling in love? And then there was the death of his brother. Wanting to find whoever had killed him had become so entwined in everything he did that Joe could hardly see past it anymore.

"Thomas has been dead for three years," she continued. "And yet the case closed without my ever really getting all the answers. I somehow have managed to come to the point where I could accept everything that happened. But now…it's all being drudged up again. And the bottom line…" She paused. "The bottom line is I'm scared. Scared of what might happen to my sister and to me. I guess I just want all of this to be over, but I also know that running won't help. But if I don't run…I don't know. I feel like a sitting duck right now."

Yellow lights reflected off the bridge on the dark water as they approached the river. As much as he wanted to, he knew he couldn't promise that everything would turn out okay.

"My mother used to always tell me I was destined to save the world. I was always rooting for the underdog and believing everyone deserved justice. Both the good guys and the bad guys." They passed a man playing a violin for change. He tossed in a couple coins as they walked by, unexpectedly stirred by the both the music and Talia's company. "Sometimes the biggest struggle for me comes when you can't save everyone. When you can't stop bad things from happening. It makes you vulnerable and, yes, even scared."

"Maybe that's why God is trying to teach me, that there are always going to be both good and bad in this world. That sometimes bad things happen to good people. That loss is as much a part of life as love is."

"I understand loss, but I know that losing a sibling can't compare to losing a spouse—"

"No, but you get how hard it is. How life will never quite be the same without that person. I guess it helps knowing that. I found that not everyone knows how to deal with loss or how to help someone else through it."

"And now?"

"I can see that God's heart was breaking along with mine. That death was never a part of His original plan, but instead a result of a fallen world." She let out a low laugh and shook her head. "Sorry. I didn't mean to be so philosophical. I'm usually not so serious, but this situation has managed to pull me back to a place I'm not sure I want to be."

"Trust me. You have nothing to be sorry about."

He kept walking, wondering how he'd allowed himself to let things get so personal. But she was the kind of person he could hold a deep conversation with and come away challenged. It was what he'd missed.

He was right that losing a brother wasn't the same as losing a spouse, but it was still loss. He understood that there were triggers that transported people back to that place of darkness. That even after all these years and the healing she'd gone through, it was normal for her to struggle with Thomas's death.

"And that other side of grief. Do you feel like you've found it yet?"

"Yes. Not that it's vanished completely, but there is joy and a renewed sense of living and purpose."

"I'm sorry for what you've had to go through. Losing a husband is hard enough. Knowing how he died and what he was involved in had to magnify the loss."

"It did. But enough about me. Tell me more about your brother. Were you close?"

He shifted his thoughts back to Ryan. It was still hard to believe he'd been gone already for three months. Sometimes it felt as if it was just yesterday when he'd last seen him.

"It was only the two of us growing up, so while we fought as kids, we became close later on. My parents always wanted more children— I'm assuming some girls—but instead they got stuck with two active boys who pushed the limits and challenged them every waking moment."

Talia laughed. "Why am I not surprised?"

"He was always adventurous. He loved travel, reading fantasy and sci-fi. Oh, and he was a huge New York Yankees fan."

She slowed down beside him, and he compensated to match her steps. "It's beautiful out here, isn't it? All the lights illuminating the old buildings."

"I've traveled some, but this is topping my list of favorite places to visit."

"Wait until you see it in the daylight. The architecture, statues and churches. There is also an incredible panoramic view from Michelangelo Square. I wish I had time to take you there today."

"Maybe someday."

Because he enjoyed seeing the world from her point of view. Things that he might simply walk by and miss. And it wasn't just because she was a tour guide. There was a passion in her voice as she talked. But the reality of what they were dealing with was evident in her voice, as well. And it brought with it a reminder of what they were facing.

"Would you like to stop somewhere and eat?" he asked, needing a distraction. "I don't know about you, but I'm starved."

"I'm not really hungry, but there's a place nearby that serves pizza and pasta late."

He glanced at her profile as they started down the narrow street toward the restaurant. He knew she was scared. He was used to deal-

ing with criminal cases, but she was an artist.
A tour guide with a love of travel and history.
She wasn't used to dealing with threats on her
life. Which meant he was going to have to do
everything in his power to keep her safe.

EIGHT

Talia glanced at her cell phone in the darkened hotel room. It was just before six in the morning. So much for a good night's sleep. She'd been awake since three and had only managed to doze on and off since then. And she'd desperately needed the rest. Her body felt exhausted from both the lack of sleep and the stress. But her mind hadn't been able to stop running. Too much had changed over the past twenty-four hours. Including having Joe Bryant in her life.

Sitting across from him in the quiet atmosphere the night before had given her a few minutes to almost forget why they were here. Almost. But nothing could erase the events of the day.

It was impossible not to bring up the past. Doing so was like pulling the scab off an old wound. It hurt. And just when she'd begun to feel as if she could stop running and move on with her life.

With someone like Joe.

She dismissed the surprising thought and stared up at the now familiar ceiling. When she hadn't been sleeping, she'd been praying. Or worrying. She was worried about her sister. Worried about the threats against her own life. Worried about what would happen if she couldn't find the paintings.

Her mother used to remind her not to worry. That today's troubles were enough without adding to them. But she'd always struggled putting that advice into practice.

You know my struggles, God. But I have no idea how to deal with this situation. No idea how not to worry.

Her faith had wavered after Thomas had died. She'd kept praying. Kept trying to find answers when there didn't seem to be any. She'd gone to church, hardly missing a service, but at the same time she couldn't help but wonder how she'd ended up where she was. She'd prayed before marrying him and thought she was doing the right thing. When she found out who he really was it was impossible to deny she'd made such a big mistake. It didn't seem possible that she hadn't even known him at all. She knew that now.

And it was that knowledge that had made her cautious over falling in love again. Having someone like Joe show up and come to her rescue like a knight in shining armor didn't change anything. Not really. She couldn't let it.

Her phone rang, and her heart took another nosedive, as she worried it was going to be more bad news. She fumbled to find it in the dark on the table beside the bed.

"Joe?"

"Hey...did I wake you?"

"No. Is everything okay?"

"Yes. I've just been laying here half the night."

"I haven't been able to sleep either," she said.

"Had a feeling I wasn't the only one. I know it's early, but I could use a walk and a bit of fresh air."

"I can be ready in ten."

He was right about the fresh air. Fifteen minutes later, she was walking down the streets of Florence, thankful for both the crisp morning and a new perspective. And for the moment, it was almost possible to pretend she was nothing more than a guide giving a private tour of the city.

"I told you it was even more beautiful in the daylight. One of my favorite cities all wrapped up in incredible architecture, history and art. And then there's the bridges, the cobblestone sidewalks and the food."

"When did you first come here?"

"I was seven, maybe eight. My sister always preferred science to history, but I couldn't get enough of my father's stories. He was a history professor, and loved talking about how the Medicis used to walk across the bridge up ahead, the Ponte Vecchio, from their palace to their offices, to ensure they didn't mix with the commoners. More than six hundred years of history. It's almost impossible to comprehend, but then you think about the birthplace of the Renaissance, the final resting place of Galileo, Ghiberti and Michelangelo. So many incredible things happened right here."

"I think I would have enjoyed meeting him."

"And I think he would have liked you, as well."

She felt a blush cross her cheeks at the implication, then couldn't help but look up at him. Strong jawline, deep brown eyes. He was staring out across the water, soaking up Florence's beauty. The breeze off the Arno River was perfect, especially knowing that in a few hours the heat from the summer sun would be radiating off the old stone paving.

She glanced away. He reminded her of Thomas. Of the things she'd first fallen in love with. His strength. His love for justice. His fight to make the world a better place. Beyond that, though, the similarities ended.

Not that she was comparing.

She turned away and focused her attention back to the scene in front of them. Four rowers skimmed across the water in perfect unison in their quad scull. A white gull soared across the top of the water. She never got tired of the old bridges scattered throughout Europe. London's Tower Bridge, Pont Neuf in Paris and the Ponte Vecchio right here in Florence. She glanced once more at Joe. And the man standing next to her simply added to the peace of the moment. Even if it was the calm before the next storm hit.

"I wonder if they're training," she asked, taking her thoughts back in check. "The rowers, I mean."

"Believe it or not, I actually dreamed of getting to the Olympics."

"Really?" She glanced up at him, thankful for the distraction from her thoughts. "What sport?"

"I was a long-distance runner in high school and college and loved it. I decided to see if I could make it to the Olympic team trials, but in the end, I missed the qualifying mark by a second."

"Yikes. That had to be tough to swallow."

"It was. At first. But then I realized that while it would have been an incredible experience, it would have pretty much engulfed my life, and I wasn't sure I was willing to give everything up for it."

"And you decided on the FBI?"

"Not at first. At that point, I just knew I was going to go into a branch of law enforcement. My grandfather was a police officer for thirty years and my father is a firefighter. I ended up graduating with a degree in criminology, and then at twenty-three I decided to apply for the FBI. What about you? Do you ever have any huge dreams?"

She stopped along the stone wall running parallel to the river and watched the gull swoop up something to eat. "I've always wanted see my art in a big gallery in some European city. But after studying all the masterpieces, it makes you feel pretty small. This is the city where I took classes and studied the frescoes in the historic center. It was an incredible experience that I wouldn't trade for the world, even if my art never gets into any of the galleries."

"I'd still like to see some of your work."

She started walking again. It had been a long time since she'd pulled out any of her pieces. "Maybe one day."

She liked the idea that they'd see each other after all of this was over. Because he was the kind of man she'd like to spend the rest of her life with. Except hadn't she thought the same thing with Thomas? He'd come in and swept her off her feet. She'd fallen in love with him, but now…his betrayal had changed everything. Which meant it really didn't matter what her heart felt. She knew that any feelings she thought she was feeling were nothing more than a recipe for disaster. And a place her heart shouldn't want to go.

Her foot hit an uneven spot in the pavement and twisted her ankle. She grabbed on to his arm in order to catch her balance. He caught her, and ran his arm around her waist to steady her.

"Sorry."

She rested her hand against his chest for a moment, then quickly pulled it away.

"You okay?" he asked.

"Yeah, I'm fine. I just…"

She didn't finish her sentence. She was close enough she could feel his breath against her cheek. He was close enough to kiss her. She ducked her head, then stepped back, her heart racing at his nearness.

He shook his head. "I'm sorry. You'd think I already learned my lesson."

"What do you mean?"

"Nothing… We probably should go get ready to catch the train."

They started walking again, but something about the morning had lost its charm.

"Who was she?"

He frowned at her question. "Who said it was a she?"

"No one, but I don't know…it sounded personal."

"Let's just say I learned never to mix business with pleasure. No matter how intense the situation becomes."

"So she was someone you rescued?" She was probing, and she probably shouldn't, but she couldn't help it. "Someone involved in one of your cases."

"Yeah, but it was a long time ago."

She wanted to ask more. Wanted to know who she'd been. Had he loved her? Had she betrayed him? But she wasn't going to. She had her own past to wrestle with.

Aside from Thomas's betrayal, she knew what it was like to love someone and worry about him going out on the job every day. She never again wanted to experience not knowing if the person she loved was going to come home at night. Or receiving the call saying that he wouldn't.

Joe wanted to kick himself as they turned down another side street toward the river and their hotel. He'd come so close to kissing her. He'd wanted to kiss her, and yet he'd meant what he said. He had no business mixing business with pleasure. And he certainly had no desire to talk about Natasha.

He turned his attention to his surroundings where there was already a busy mixture of locals and tourists. Cars and mopeds rushed by. The last thing he needed right now was a distraction. He pushed away any fleeting feelings of attraction. He knew better. Not that he believed she was involved in a crime, like Natasha was. But even that didn't matter.

He knew how things worked. She might be innocent in this situation, but when all this was over he'd never see her again. He wasn't her knight in shining armor, sweeping into save the day. He was an FBI agent looking to take down a thief and the person who murdered his brother. Nothing more. Nothing less.

The sharp crack of a gunshot jerked him out of his thoughts.

Joe reacted automatically. "Talia, get down! Now."

He thought the shot had come from behind him, but he couldn't be certain. With a brick wall running along the river to their right and an open street to their left, they were sitting ducks. He grabbed Talia's hand and started running. In an outdoor situation, the best response was to look for both cover and distance, with the goal being to put as much distance between the shooter and the target.

And he was certain they were the target.

"Joe…" She squeezed his fingers as they ran. "Joe—you've been hit."

He glanced down at the trail of blood that was spreading across the sleeve of his T-shirt and running down his arm. Another few inches to the left, and he wouldn't still be standing. But there was no time to go through what could have happened. "It doesn't matter."

Not now. Adrenaline masked the pain. All

he could feel was his heart racing and the fierce determination of getting her to safety.

The street was in a state of confusion. Those who had heard the shot were running for cover. Others didn't even react. Cars continued to drive through the intersection, unaware of what was going on, which meant they had to run through oncoming traffic in order to get to any semblance of safety.

There was another shot and the sound of glass shattering one of the windows of a car behind them. The shots were coming from northwest of them, but he still couldn't locate the shooter.

"We need to find cover. Don't stop running."

NINE

Joe blocked out the pain radiating down his arm as they ran and focused instead on both identifying the shooter and finding an exit strategy. Most people, when faced with a clearly imminent threat, tended to freeze. But that reaction could mean valuable seconds lost, giving the attacking force an advantage. Years of training made his own response automatic. Which meant unlike an everyday victim in a similar scenario, he was already seconds ahead in his thinking.

But this situation was more complex than simply deciding the best way to take down an active shooter. His first priority—his only priority at the moment—was keeping Talia safe. Which meant he had to get her away from the attacker.

"Joe—"

"Just keep running."

From where they were, the closest cover was in one of the shops across the street, but the last thing he wanted was to be boxed in without an escape route.

The other option was the covered bridge straight ahead.

He glanced briefly behind him without slowing down. Fifty feet behind them he caught sight of the shooter. A figure wearing a gray sweatshirt and a ball cap, and carrying a weapon, was coming toward them. Male, female, age—he couldn't tell. But what bothered him the most was that the person wasn't acting logically. Why shoot at them in broad daylight, with dozens of potential witnesses? It meant that either the gunman was panicked, or they believed they were invincible and could manage to escape. And it meant they were willing to take risks in achieving their objective.

Making sure his body was between her and the shooter, Joe gripped Talia's hand tighter and picked up their pace, wondering where he'd faltered. Taking in his surroundings had become second nature to him. He always knew where the nearest exit was at a restaurant or store. Always looked for anything or anyone that didn't fit into his environment.

Today, though, he'd managed to get caught

up in the moment and missed the warning that they were in immediate danger. But there was no time for regrets. He'd have to deal with those later. Instead he made his decision. Their best option was to get to the bridge. The problem, though, was that it was still another ninety to one hundred feet ahead of them and their sniper was still behind them. Which meant the odds of finding cover before getting shot weren't good.

He kept running toward the bridge. The sound of gunshots had sent dozens of people scurrying for cover and ducking into shops. And even though it was early, there was still a steady stream of cars going past, putting frightened pedestrians at risk of getting hit on top of getting shot. But for the moment, the only thing he could focus on was getting Talia to safety.

His gut churned with unease. Until they got to the bridge and were able to find cover, they were in reality pinned down and completely vulnerable. But as long as the person with the gun was also moving, the odds of him hitting his target accurately were going to be far lower. Which was why they had to keep moving.

Someone yelled behind them. He had no idea what was being shouted beyond *polizia*. He glanced back, searching quickly once again, but he couldn't find the shooter this time.

Where is he, God?

He still had to be nearby. Lurking in the shadows. Trying to blend in with the swarm of terrified tourists. But there was no way he'd get away with this. Someone had to have seen him shooting and would be able to ID him. And at this point the sniper's only escape was one of the side streets away from the river.

Joe shifted his focus back to the bridge. Seventy-five more feet… Fifty…

He kept running.

"Joe, where is he?"

He caught the panic in her voice. "I don't know. I lost him. We just need to make it to the bridge."

He searched the crowd across the street. No one suspicious there, which meant he still had to be behind them.

They reached the edge of the bridge where the Ponte Vecchio spanned the Arno River at the narrowest point. Instead of being open like most European bridges, this one had dozens of overhanging shops that dated back to the Roman era. The perfect location, he hoped, for evasion.

"This way," he said, leading her onto the bridge.

"Joe, you're bleeding too much."

"Maybe, but we can't take a chance of stopping and one of us getting shot again."

His heart raced inside his chest. His arm was beginning to throb despite the adrenaline pumping through his body that should have helped mask the impact of the bullet. Ignoring the pain, he led her across the bridge, where shops were just beginning to open up. Past wooden doorways and shop windows. Past store after store selling jewelry and gold, sprinkled with a few places selling postcards and gelato.

"Do you see him?" she asked.

He glanced behind them again, trying to sort through the blur of people on the bridge as he searched for the figure in the gray sweatshirt. "No, but keep running."

Some people glanced oddly at them, but most were headed in the opposite direction to see what was happening on the street.

In the center of the stone bridge, archways opened up to stunning views of the Arno River. He could hear sirens wailing in the background. Someone had called the authorities. He was going to have to make his own call and let his boss know what had happened. He also needed to let Esposito know what was going on, and in return get an update on last night's train incident. There had to be a connection between the woman who'd followed them and what was happening right now. He needed her ID'd and brought in. And they needed to find the paintings that were the reason for all of this.

"We have to stop," she said, grabbing on to his good arm. She slowed down in front of one of the shops, and grabbed on to his uninjured arm. Rows of gold necklaces sat lined up on display. "I meant it when I said you were bleeding too much. If you keep pushing it, you won't make it much farther."

"I'm fine. We need to get as far from here as possible." Just because they were on the bridge didn't mean he was ready to stop. Not yet. They could catch a taxi on the other side that would take them out of the neighborhood and somewhere safe.

"You're losing too much blood," she said. "Besides, I'm pretty sure our shooter's disappeared."

He drew in a deep breath. Maybe she was right. He could feel himself slowing down. His legs were beginning to feel like lead, and he was struggling to get enough air.

You're fine. It's nothing but a flesh wound, which means you'll be back on your feet as soon as you can catch your breath.

At least that's what he kept trying to tell himself. Whoever had shot him might not have had the best aim, or maybe they'd done exactly what they'd wanted to do—make sure he was pulled off the case without actually killing him. He wasn't sure which made more sense. But what he was sure about was that even a bullet wasn't going to stop him at this point.

Talia pulled him inside. She started speaking rapidly in Italian to a woman behind a glass display. Something about the police and a gun. The woman replied, speaking even faster. He took a step forward, but the room was spinning. Funny. He'd never had issues with vertigo. Boats, planes, cars—nothing bothered him, but this… A wave of nausea hit him, along with a sharp pain that radiated to his fingertips.

"Joe—Joe, I need you to sit down."

"I'm fine." He was still determined to shake it off.

"No, you're not, which is why right now all

you need to think about is going to the hospital."

Maybe she was right after all. He couldn't stop the dizziness. There were two of her. Two heads, four eyes... The room was spinning. He tried to shake it off. He needed to protect her. That was why he was here. To protect her from whoever was trying to kill them.

Talia refused to give in to panic. She took a deep breath and guided Joe to the back of the room.

"Joe," she said. "I'm calling for an ambulance. You're going to be fine, but I need you to take deep slow deep breaths and relax. We need to elevate your arm above your heart."

She turned back to the woman, who was still standing in the middle of the store, unsure of how to react to two people barging into her store, one who was bleeding on her floor. "I need you to lock the front door and put up the Closed sign in case we were followed," she said to her in Italian.

The woman hesitated. "You think the shooter might follow you here?"

"I don't know, but please. I'm not trying to put you in danger, and I can't be certain, but we do need your help. Please."

She tapped her heel, then glanced at the door. "Okay. I will help you."

"He needs to lie down," Talia said.

"There's a place in the back of the room," she said, leading them behind the counter.

Joe didn't move. "I really don't need to lie down."

He was fighting with her again. Acting agitated and anxious. All signs of shock.

"Joe, you kept me safe out there. Now it's my turn to ensure your safety. Trust me. You're not fine. You need to lie down."

He shook his head. "Burns like fire, but I don't think it's serious."

"I'll be the judge of that." She turned to the woman. "Can you get me something to help stop the bleeding? A towel…anything you might have."

"I think I can come up with some hand towels."

She turned back to Joe while the woman searched for the towels. "You can lie here behind the counter until the ambulance gets here."

"Talia—"

"I tell you, I've never met such a stubborn man," she said. "Lie down and be still."

"I just don't want someone else getting shot."

"It's a bit late for that, and you've played enough superhero for today. So before you pass out on me, lie down."

Seconds later she had Joe on the floor and his arm elevated. The clerk handed her two small white towels. She immediately pressed them both against the wound.

Sirens blared in the distance. At least she hadn't heard any more shots. But that didn't mean they were out of the woods yet. She brushed her free hand across Joe's forehead. His skin was clammy, his face had paled, and his pulse was rapid. She glanced down at the towel. Blood had already turned it red.

She pressed harder against the wound. Her medical expertise ended with Band-Aids and ankle braces. She knew more facts about Florence than how to treat a gunshot wound. How the city had become the first in all of Europe to have paved streets. How Leonardo Da Vinci had been born here in 1452. Or how the Duoma—a domed cathedral—had 463 stone steps that led to a stunning view of the city.

Dealing with this type of wound hadn't exactly been a part of her education. Or how to deal with an active shooter. And the only way she knew to keep herself from panicking was to hold on to facts and the small sliver of reality that was left.

"Did you know that this bridge was the only bridge along the Arno River that wasn't blown up by the Germans? Charles Steinhauslin convinced one of the German generals not to blow it up because of its historical value and it worked."

Joe just stared up at her. "What?"

"The bridge we're on. The Ponte Vecchio. It's…never mind. I ramble when I'm stressed. I start spewing out facts and other nonsense. It's an annoying habit, or so I've been told."

But that wasn't what had her worried.

"Joe, there's something else. The bleeding isn't stopping, and I don't know what else to do other than elevate your arm and keep pressure on it."

"Then we have a problem. It should have slowed down by now." Joe switched his gaze to his arm. "In order to stop the bleeding, I think you're going to have to press on the brachial artery."

"Okay. Where is that?"

"Right below my armpit. Grab underneath my arm, wrap your fingers along the inner part and then press firmly. When you've got the right place, the bleeding should slow down."

"How do you know that?" she said, working quickly to follow his instructions."

"Training. There are a lot of things you don't know about me."

"Like?"

"After spending half a dozen summers as a lifeguard throughout high school and college, one of the things I wanted to be growing up was a doctor. I ended up taking a bunch of first aid on the side."

"Anything else I should be doing then?" she asked.

"Do you notice any rapid swelling around the wound?"

"No...what would that mean?"

"Internal bleeding." Her stomach clenched at the reality of the situation started to hit her. She wasn't sure about internal bleeding, but she did know that no matter where the bullet had hit, it was going to cause damage.

She'd do anything to be back in Rome talking to a bunch of rowdy tourists instead of on the run from a crazed sniper with connections to her husband's death. Her life had truly been turned upside down.

She glanced again at the door, wishing she knew what was going on outside. "Tell me this was just a random shooting, and we were in the wrong place at the wrong time."

He shook his head, wincing as she pressed against his arm, but at least he seemed calmer. "I wish, but that would be way too much of a coincidence with all that's happened the past few days."

"So you think they were trying to kill you?"

"I don't know, but I'm pretty sure whoever is behind this wants me out of the picture. This was just supposed to be you searching for the paintings, remember. No authorities in the picture. And now they know I'm with you."

"How do they know you're part of law enforcement?"

"On the train, I told the woman I was FBI. She—or whoever's behind this—wants you to have to deal with this on your own. And so there's no chance of me confiscating the paintings once—if—we find them."

"Maybe you're right, but that's pretty risky, shooting at a government agent. Especially since whoever is behind this probably isn't even from here."

"I agree, but I think they panicked. And when you're that scared you make foolish choices. Like going after your target in broad daylight."

"How's the bleeding?" he asked, looking down at his arm.

"I think it's finally slowing."

Her pulse was racing. Her own breathing labored. If anything happened to him… She tried to ignore the feelings brought on by that thought. But she'd seen how he'd looked at her when they were standing together next to the river. And she'd felt her own reaction to his nearness. And how for a moment she'd actually wished that he would have kissed her.

But this wasn't about him being her hero and coming to her rescue. She already decided that she was never going to date a lawman again. Thomas had betrayed her, but his death had really driven home that his job had been dangerous. And so was Joe's. And that wasn't something she was going to deal with again.

The store clerk was back again, hovering beside Talia. "Can I get you anything else?"

"What about the ambulance?" she answered back in Italian.

"It should be here in less than five minutes." The store clerk glanced at the window. "I just called my brother, who has a shop down the road. He said he saw the shooter."

"What's happening?" Joe asked Talia.

"There's an ambulance on its way right now."

"Someone had to have gotten a good look at him," Joe said. "Though from what I saw it could have been a man or a woman from the way they were dressed."

"The police are here," the woman said, running toward the door and unlocking it.

Three police officers marched through the door, followed by two paramedics and a gurney.

Talia stood up and moved back, giving them room behind the counter to get to where Joe lay. "Please tell me he's going to be all right."

"Looks like he's lost a lot of blood, but we'll take care of him."

She turned to one of the officers while Joe was settled onto the gurney. "Have you found the shooter?"

"We've secured the bridge and surrounding areas and have a description, but we're going to need your statement."

"I need to go with him to the hospital first... please."

"Tell them I'm with the FBI," Joe said to Talia. "Give them Esposito's number so he can update them on what's going on."

Talia gave the officers the number off Joe's

phone, thanked the store clerk, then followed the paramedics outside the shop and toward the other side of the bridge, where the ambulance was waiting. A crowd had gathered, watching as she hurried to keep up.

Her phone went off as soon as she sat down in the back of the ambulance. She hesitated, then pulled it out of her back pocket to read the message.

Do you know why this happened? It's your fault. I told you not to involve the authorities and now your friend will die. All because you didn't listen.

Talia stared at the text. Joe had been right. This was all because of her. And if he died, she would be the reason for his death.

TEN

Talia paced the freshly waxed floor of the emergency room. As soon as they'd arrived by ambulance, news of a gunshot victim had sent the staff running. Joe had been given a priority code number that had put him in the front of the line and immediately in to see a surgeon. She glanced at her phone for the hundredth time. It was already after noon. Well over three hours since they'd arrived. And over an hour since anyone had given her an update, which had her stress level soaring.

But Joe's situation wasn't the only reason she was so upset.

As far as she knew, whoever had shot Joe was still out there.

A roomful of people sat on hard, plastic chairs. A television played the news. A baby cried in the background. She glanced at the doors leading outside. She'd given her statement to the police shortly after their arrival, which had let to more questions, most of them still unanswered as far as she was concerned. But she had no idea if they'd found the gunman. Or the woman on the train. Which had her jumping every time the doors opened.

Because how hard would it be to track them down to this hospital? Whoever had shot Joe would try again. But surely not here, right? It was a possibility, though. The person behind this was making some twisted decisions, so Talia wasn't sure what might happen next.

She looked down at her hands and rubbed her fingers together. She'd scrubbed them in the restroom, trying to wash away Joe's blood. Wishing she could as easily wash away the memories of the past few days. Asking herself how her life had managed to spiral out of control so quickly. And now if something happened to Joe, if he didn't make it... She gulped in a lungful of air. She'd known that getting the bleeding to stop—along with getting him to the hospital—increased his chances of survival, but while he'd been lucid when they'd taken him away, she knew there could be no guarantees at this point.

She took a sip of the bottled water she'd bought a few minutes earlier, then thought back once again to that moment on the bridge when she'd been convinced he was going to kiss her. And despite all her hard work to guard her heart she felt that same undeniable attraction. But she couldn't let that guard down now. Not when she was only caught up in a wave of emotions. That's all this draw toward him was. She was vulnerable, scared, and he'd been the one who'd come to her rescue.

Like Thomas had always done until he'd decided to risk everything they had together and lost.

No. She wasn't ever going through that again.

I know there's nothing I can do, God, beyond leaving this situation to You, but this is all still so hard.

Even finding the strength to trust wasn't easy. Not God. Not Joe…and certainly not her heart.

She started pacing again, hating the feeling of being out of control. She knew the risks someone like Joe faced. He might be after white-collar criminals and art thieves, but that didn't make him immune to danger. Today had made that clear. And the thought of giving her heart away to someone like that… Well, that wasn't happening.

She stared at the double doors where they'd

taken him and wondered how long it was going to be until they gave her an update. She glanced at her phone She needed to let her brother-in-law know what was going on. If they did get to Venice today, which was becoming less likely, it was going to be late. Which meant the easiest thing to do was get a couple of hotel rooms and meet up with Marco in the morning. She punched in his number, waited for him to answer, then ended up leaving him a message.

She disconnected the call as a text came in from her sister.

Are you okay? I don't think I'll be able to sleep until this is over.

It was around six in the morning in Dallas.

She started to call her sister, then stopped when one of the nurses approached her.

"You're with Mr. Bryant, the gunshot victim, right?" she asked in Italian.

Talia's heart raced as she dropped her phone into her pocket. "Yes."

"I'm sorry it's taken us so long to get back to you. This place has been crazy today. We're having trouble having enough beds for everyone."

"How is he?"

"He's going to need to stay a while longer, but he's asking for you. You can come with me and see him if you'd like."

Talia hesitated before following the woman. "Is he going to be okay?"

"As with any gunshot wound, he's fortunate to be alive, but the bullet passed through and tissue damage is minimal. The doctor wants him to wait here a couple more hours so we can watch his vitals while waiting for the results of the CT scan. But as long as there is no further damage, it looks like after a few days of rest and a round of strong antibiotics, he'll be okay."

Talia blew out a sharp breath with the relief that came with the woman's assurance, then followed her through the double doors,

Joe was sitting on the edge of the bed, shirtless and his arm bandaged.

"Hey," she said, slipping into the room. She set down a package she'd picked up while she'd been waiting, then pulled out the Firenze, Italia T-shirt she'd bought in the small hospital store. "I know it's a bit touristy, but I thought you might need a new shirt."

And at least he was alive. That was all that seemed to matter at the moment.

He smiled up at her and nodded at the gift. "Thanks."

"How are you feeling?"

"The pain medicine finally kicked in, so I'm feeling a bit better."

"The nurse told me it was a clean shot."

"I'm going to be sore for a while, but it could have been a lot worse."

She tightened her grip around the empty bag in an attempt to calm her jumpy nerves. There had been enough lives lost. It had to stop.

"Do you know how often a train leaves for Venice?" he asked.

Her eyes widened. "Why? Because you're not leaving Florence."

"I'm not staying. We need to find those paintings—"

"I have a feeling the doctor isn't going to agree."

"The surgeon was able to stop the bleeding and repair most of the damage. As soon as they confirm the results of the CT scan, we can grab our stuff at the hotel and leave for Venice."

Talia frowned at Joe's stubbornness. Did he seriously think he could keep going like nothing had happened? "I was told you needed a few more days of rest before you do anything.

Because in case you missed it somehow, you were just wounded by a bullet."

"Funny." He shot her an annoyed look. "But I don't exactly have an option. Last time I looked we were running out of time to get the paintings. Resting isn't going to speed up that time line. I'm already frustrated I have to hang around here as long as I've had to."

"There are other options. There's still me."

"Meaning?"

"I'll go on to Venice and find the paintings while you stay here and recover."

"Not a chance," he said. "That's what whoever did this wants. And it's not happening."

"Joe—"

"I'm serious, Talia. There's no way you're going there by yourself."

"What about your arm? You're not going to do me any good if you're not well."

"My arm will be fine, and like I said, time isn't exactly on our side. I've got antibiotics and pain medicine. I've had worse injuries."

She wanted to argue with him. Ask him what injury he'd had that had been worse than this. But if she was honest with herself, she didn't want to get on that train by herself, and she had no illusions of trying to prove to him that she was some kind of superwoman. Because she wasn't. And the thought of going to Venice, even with Joe, had her panic level soaring. He'd just been shot to apparently get him out of the way. What were they going to do to her if she didn't get them what they wanted? As far as she was concerned this had turned into a lose-lose situation.

"So what are you proposing?"

"As soon as they let me out, we head back to the hotel, get something to eat and then catch the train to Venice."

She mentally weighed their options. It would be late when they got there. She hadn't been able to get a hold of her brother-in-law, but she knew that the neighbor had a key and they could always rent a couple rooms at a hotel. It was high season, but they should be able to find something.

"What about your contact with the Carabinieri? Esposito. What if he came with me?"

"He's willing to help out, but he's stuck down south working a case and can't get away for at least forty-eight hours."

"And your boss? What does he say?"

Joe frowned. "I haven't talked to him today."

"Maybe you need to. Maybe he could send someone else. Because clearly someone wants you off this case. And next time you might not

end up in the emergency room. You—or I—
could end up in the morgue."

The sun had just set over the medieval city
as Joe walked through the train station next to
Talia a few hours later, tickets in his hand for
the next train to Venice. He hoped he'd made
the right decision. He glanced at her solemn expression beside him. He knew she was scared.
And he couldn't blame her. The past twenty-four
hours had taken a toll on both of them, physically and mentally. But he had no intention of
pulling out. Not yet. The memory of his brother's death still lingered too freshly in his mind,
along with the all too real threats she was facing. He didn't want to risk Talia's life, but he
needed answers and this was the only way he
knew how to get them. "You still sure about
this?" she asked as she took the tickets and val-
idated them before they headed for the train.

He ignored the fatigue running through him.
"What I am sure about is that we don't have a
lot of options at this point."

She glanced at his bandaged arm. "And if
they've managed to follow us onto this train
again?"

"If you're wondering if I can still take them

down—" he shot her a smile "—you'd be surprised what I can do with only one good arm."

She gave him a smile as she headed toward the doors of one of the train cars. "The thought had crossed my mind."

"The pain's tolerable. I'll be fine."

"You just need to make sure you keep taking your pain medicine so you can keep it under control."

He nodded, but he'd rather tolerate the pain then down a bunch of pain medicine that kept him from functioning. He needed to be completely alert and not let his guard down.

He couldn't let her sidetrack him, either, because as far as he was concerned, Talia was a distraction. A big one. And one that had him wondering while sitting in the emergency room what it would be like to let his heart feel again. It was something he hadn't considered for so long, but there was something about her that had made him what to get to know her better. To see if those initial sparks he'd felt were ones that could turn into something deeper.

But that was a place he wasn't going to allow himself to go. He'd sensed the interest in her eyes as they'd walked along the Arno River. Felt it deepen the moment when he'd almost leaned downed and kissed her. But that would have been a mistake. Mixing the high intensity of his job with a relationship. He couldn't go there.

He reined in his thoughts and studied the train platform, his senses on high alert. A family of four—clearly tourists—struggled with too many suitcases. A handful of businessmen and students, a couple of families... This wasn't about his feelings for Talia. It was about finding who'd killed his brother. And about ensuring Talia's safety. Nothing more. Nothing less. And that frame of mind was where he planned to stay. The lives of both of them depended on it.

They stepped onto the train. They'd disposed of the tracking device, but he still searched for anyone who looked either familiar or suspicious. He wasn't about to take any chances.

"Heard from your brother-in-law yet?" he asked, slipping into his seat.

"It keeps going straight to voice mail, which is strange. I've left a couple of messages. Not sure there's much more I can do at this point."

Joe's phone rang as Talia sat down beside him.

"Joe, this is Antonio Esposito. I've been working with the local police regarding the shooting, but I wanted to find out personally how you were doing."

His hand went automatically to his injured arm. "It's been a bit crazy today."

"Are you okay?"

"Just sore, and have to watch for infection, but fortunately the doctor was able to repair most of the damage."

"Where are you now?"

"On my way to Venice."

"Wait a minute…you were just shot and the doctor let you leave?"

"I can be pretty persuasive."

"Stubborn is more like it. You shouldn't be out there, Joe. I might be able to get away in the next day or two and take over the case—"

"We don't have a day or two. And there's no doubt that whoever is behind this is serious. I wouldn't be doing this if I couldn't handle it physically. But we need to put an end to this."

"They might be serious, but they're also desperate. A shooting in broad daylight?"

"What do you know about that? Have they found the gunman?"

"Not yet, but they're going to make a mistake. I've made sure that the police know what's going on. They're going to find whoever did this."

"There's another reason I called. I've got some more information on the man who broke in to Signora Morello's apartment. Matteo Arena."

"What have you got?"

"He's been in and out of prison over the past few years, mainly for theft and a couple of assaults."

"Has he told you who hired him?"

"No. Only that he was to follow Signora Morello and ensure she found the paintings."

"Why grab her bag at the Colosseum?"

"He said he thought she'd changed her mind when she headed toward home and away from the meeting place. He didn't want to risk losing them if they were on her. As soon as I can get free, I'm planning to see what I can get out of him."

"Call me if you get anything else. We'll be in Venice tonight, and I'm hoping by tomorrow we'll have the paintings." He glanced at Talia, who sat staring out the window. "One more thing. What about the woman on the train? Have you been able to ID her yet from the photo?"

"Not yet, but I'll let you know when we do."

Talia turned to him as soon as he hung up. "What did he say?"

"They've been interrogating the guy who broke in to your apartment."

"And?"

He gave her a rundown of their conversation.

Her frown deepened as he finished. "You said something about a photo of the woman on the train. What photo?"

"I thought I told you. I took one on my phone while I was walking past her pretending to text."

"No. I didn't know."

"I'm sorry. I thought I showed you."

"Can I see it?"

He found the image, then handed her his phone.

Talia seemed to zoom in on the woman's face and stared at it.

"What is it?" he asked.

"I'm not sure. She looks familiar."

"How? Like someone from the Colosseum?"

"I'm not sure. There's something about her, but I can't place her." Talia zoomed in on the scar above the woman's eyebrow. "Wait a minute… Change her hair color and the style, give her less makeup, fifteen or so fewer pounds, and place her in an entirely different setting…"

"You know her?"

"Yes." Talia grabbed his hand and looked up at him. "Her name's Anna Hayes. She was Thomas's partner when he was on the force."

ELEVEN

A wave of nausea mingled with fear washed over Talia at the recognition of the woman. She shifted in her seat. Thomas had trusted Anna with his life. If she knew about the paintings she had to have been involved.

But how?

"Are you sure that's her?" Joe asked.

"Yes." She nodded, wishing all of this made sense. "I didn't catch it at first because like I said her appearance is altered some. Even the clothes she was wearing weren't what Anna would wear, but yes…I'm sure it's her. That scar above her eyebrow, she got it on the job. Someone they were trying to arrest cracked her over the head with a beer bottle. I can't believe I didn't recognize her."

Why would Anna threaten to kill her? The ramifications of her husband's former partner's involvement were significant, bringing with them a slew of disturbing questions. What was her connection to the stolen drug money? Had she been working with Thomas?

Every scenario that surfaced made her sick.

Because she'd trusted Anna. The woman had stood beside her at Thomas's funeral. She'd called Talia to check on her. She'd been a friend. Not close, but a friend. And to think that Anna had betrayed her...

"How well did you know her?" Joe asked, breaking into her thoughts.

"She and Thomas were partners for a couple years. I considered her a friend. I always thought she was a good cop. Tough, but seemed to care about her job. Thomas trusted her with his life, and as far as I know they didn't have any issues between them."

It seemed that everything she'd known— both about Thomas and now about Anna— had been a lie.

And now Anna was somehow involved. She—like Thomas—wasn't the person Talia thought she was.

"At the time of your husband's death, were there ever any hints that she might be involved in the thefts from the raids?"

"If there was I never heard about it. Doesn't mean she wasn't questioned or that the thought didn't cross the minds of the investigators, but as far as I knew, she wasn't involved."

Talia stared at the photo a few more seconds then handed the phone back to Joe. Matteo Arena, the guy who'd broken in to her house, had told her that the person he was working for had been involved in Thomas's murder. Did that mean that Anna had killed Thomas? Had they gotten into a fight over the stolen goods and she'd ended up killing him?

She squeezed her eyes shut and took a deep breath. There were too many questions and not enough answers.

"There something else," Talia said, turning back to Joe. "If she was the one who winged you, I believe she did it on purpose."

"What do you mean?"

"I mean if she'd wanted you dead, you'd be dead right now."

Joe's expression darkened. "So she's a good shot."

"Very. She was always trying to beat Thomas during training exercises, and he was one of the department's best. It was like a long-standing rivalry between the two of them. I always thought it was crazy, not everyone in the department was like that, but they were both so competitive. Her even more so than Thomas."

"So if it was her, she wasn't trying to kill me. Instead she was trying to get me out of the picture. It's a possibility I'd thought of even before we had an idea of who the gunman could be, but now it seems more likely."

The train sped through another tunnel, darkening the car. Why would Anna shoot at an FBI agent in broad daylight? The odds of her getting caught in a situation like that were very high. Unless she really was desperate.

"She doesn't want the FBI involved," Joe said.

"So she shoots you? I'm still struggling to put this all together in my mind. I know what I just said, but it still seems far too risky, even for someone who is good with guns."

"She just has to hold things off until you get her those paintings, or until she finds them herself."

"Then if she has a buyer, she takes the millions and disappears."

"And in the meantime, she expects me to do this on my own," Talia said.

"She *needs* you to do this on your own. She said she didn't want anyone else involved. The more people tangled up in this, the greater the chances of things not going her way. She knows an FBI agent wouldn't hand over the paintings if we find them first."

The train flew out of the tunnel, then seconds later was speeding through a small rural community sprinkled with a few dozen houses with red tiled roofs.

"I remember talking to her at the funeral," Talia said. "She told me how sorry she was for my loss. Told me that despite everything that had happened, that Thomas had been a good partner. That even though he made bad choices that he still loved me. That he talked about me to her all the time." Talia stared out the window and caught her reflection, wishing she could shake the numbness. "But this... If this is her, then she's involved. Which means she lied to me. And if she lied to me about her involvement, then what else was she dishonest about?"

Her mind had played through the scenario hundreds of times since the night her husband had died. Ever since, she'd tried to figure out how she could have missed the signs that he was involved in something illegal. But no matter what she wanted to believe, she couldn't refute the evidence. Not the ten thousand dollars in cash, the other stolen evidence they'd found in Thomas's possession, or the account linked to his name.

But now she wanted to know what Anna's connection was. She had to have known something. Including who'd shot Thomas.

"What are you thinking?" he asked, breaking into her thoughts.

"That if you would have told me four, maybe five years ago, what Thomas was going to do, I never would have believed you. And yet the evidence was there. It left no doubts in my mind that my husband wasn't the man I thought he was. But this—this changes everything. Anna's involvement. I need to know the truth. Once and for all about what happened that night."

She needed to call the assistant chief.

She pulled her phone from her pocket. "I'm going to call Captain Blythe."

"Do you think that's wise? I'm not sure who we can confide in at this point."

"Who else am I supposed to trust? Not only did he call me to give me a heads-up, but he would know where she is."

Ignoring Joe's concerns, she pulled out her phone, dialed the assistant chief's number.

"Captain Blythe," she said as soon as he'd answered. "This is Talia Morello again."

"Talia…are you okay?"

"For now, but you said to call if I needed anything."

"Of course I meant it. What's going on?"

"I was just trying to get a hold of Detective Hayes and wondered if you could give me a way to contact her."

"Your husband's old partner?"

"Yeah…does she still work for the department?"

"Yes, but she's on leave, actually. Can I ask why you need to speak to her?"

"It's just for something personal." Talia hesitated, unsure of how much she should say until she could figure out exactly what was going on. "Actually, I thought I saw her here."

"In Italy?"

She pressed her lips together before continuing. "I know. It doesn't make sense, but I'm sure it was her."

"I wish I could help you, but like I said, she's not around right now. From what I understand there was a death in the family that she needed to deal with. But whoever you saw, it's probably just someone who looks like her. Anna's family lives in El Paso, not Italy. But I can pass on your cell number to her if you'd like."

"I would. Thank you. If you'd have her call me, then I'm sure we can clear things up."

Or at least she hoped this was all somehow one big mistake.

"Call me if you need anything else," he said. "Please."

"I will. Thank you."

She finished the call, then turned back to Joe.

"What did he say?" he said.

"That conveniently Anna's on leave. A death in the family. She could have lied. No one would know unless they started poking into the situation."

"Like we have?"

"It was her, Joe. It was her on the train. And I'm now convinced that she was the one who shot you. Which means she was involved in all of this somehow."

"I need to call Esposito and give him an update, see if he has anything for us." Joe glanced at his watch. "It's getting pretty late, though."

"And you look tired." She glanced at his arm. At least the wound hadn't bled through the bandage. "How's the pain?"

"On a scale from one to ten…about a five. But I'll be fine."

Maybe, but she didn't miss the fatigue in his eyes "Forget about the case for the moment. What you need is a good night's sleep before we start searching in the morning."

* * *

Just past five the next morning, Joe stared at the ceiling of his hotel room. The sun had yet to rise, but he felt as if he'd been awake for hours. And he knew that despite the pain pills he'd taken during the night he wasn't going to be able to sleep anymore because of the ache in his shoulder. He got up and went to the small sink in the bathroom and washed down two more of the pills with a bottle of water, hoping it would take the edge off the pain. Maybe Talia had been right. Maybe he was pushing it too much, but the clock was ticking, and they needed to find the paintings.

He left a message on her voice mail, asking her to meet him in the lobby when she was ready, then headed downstairs to get a strong cup of coffee.

Three cups of coffee and an hour later Talia stepped out of the elevator, looking far more awake than she had the night before when they'd arrived at the hotel. He shifted his gaze to the painting behind her, trying not to notice how nice she looked in a pink flowered dress with the hem landing just above her knees.

"Morning," he said, setting down his empty coffee cup and standing up when she reached him.

"Morning. How's your arm?"

"Still there."

"Funny. Seriously, how are you feeling? You're not exactly following the doctor's orders and resting."

"It hurts, but I took some more pain medicine and it's finally kicking in." He glanced down at his limb. "I tried to redo the dressing myself, but really, I'm fine."

"I can tell you did it yourself, and you did a terrible job. Come on." She shot him a smile, then led him toward a more private corner of the lobby. "Did you take your antibiotics?"

"Yes, ma'am," he said, pulling out a new set of dressings from his backpack.

She sat down beside him, then pulled up the sleeve of his gray button-down.

"Seriously," he said. "It's nothing."

"You keep saying that, and yet you were shot. That will always be a big deal to me."

She pulled off the old bandage.

"Ouch."

"I thought this wasn't a big deal? It's red around the edges, and if you put the cream on it, I can't see it."

"Sorry, doc."

"I suppose you get a few brownie points from your colleagues from what you've gone through. I'm assuming most FBI art agents don't run into a lot of bullets."

"You're just full of jokes this morning," he said, catching the smile in her eyes.

"Just wait until I get my morning coffee."

He laughed, wishing she didn't have to be so funny, and genuine and beautiful. They were ignoring the inevitable, but he didn't mind. Another few minutes before having to deal with the real reason they were here was fine with him.

"There," she said, stepping back. "You're good for another few hours, though if I were you, I'd have this checked out again by a real doctor in a day or two. You don't want to get an infection."

He rolled his sleeve back down. "You hungry? I think they might finally be open for breakfast."

She rested her hands against her hips. "I'm getting the impression that you're always hungry, aren't you?"

"It has to be the Italian food," he said, zipping up his backpack then standing up. "And on top of that, I'm a bachelor used to living on frozen dinners and fast food."

"That should be a crime if you ask me. They

are supposed to serve a complimentary hot breakfast, but all I want right now is coffee."

"Well, I'm starving, which has to be a good sign."

He followed her out onto a small terrace lined with flowers and lanterns, but what caught his eye was the sweeping waters of the Grand Canal dotted by dozens of boats. Its banks were lined with dozens of century-old buildings that seemed to float on the horizon of the gray blue water.

"Wow… I've traveled a lot, but this is incredible."

"I could stare at this view all day and never quite soak it all up."

"Why don't you get us a table if you're not going to eat, and I'll be right back."

He filled up his plate with eggs and bacon and a couple of pastries before joining Talia at a table with a view of the canal.

"So are you telling me you've never visited Venice?" she said, taking a sip of her coffee.

"I've been to both Rome and Florence, but never this far north."

"How can you come to Italy and not see Venice?" He saw the surprise in her eyes. "I love Rome, and Florence and even Pisa, but Venice…despite some of the memories this city brings, it will always hold a piece of my heart."

He dug into his breakfast, wondering what kind of memories the city held for her. Her husband's family was from here, which meant the time she'd spent here was far more than any tourist.

"Once again," he said, "I could really use a tour guide."

She added a package of sugar to her coffee. "I think I could arrange that when this is over. The history of this city is fascinating. Set on over a hundred small islands with dozens of canals and linked by bridges—just over four hundred, in fact. In the past it held a strategic position, commercially, but it also had enough naval power to protect the sea routes from piracy. In fact there was a time when the city was very powerful."

"I've heard the city's sinking?"

"About one to two millimeters a year. If we have time, when this is all over I'll have to give you a proper tour, including a ride out on the water on the *vaporetto*."

"The what?"

"It's a water bus." She pointed to one of the long, flat-top boats floating past. "Venice's public transportation. It might not be as romantic as the gondolas, but the views are just as good for a fraction of the price."

Joe took another bite of his breakfast. "You could start the tour now. Tell me about Venice's hold on you."

"The first time I came here was to meet Thomas's parents. They showed me around the city and some of the nearby islands. I was as captivated as I am today."

"I can see why," he said.

"I think you'd like Thomas's father. He's always telling us Italian proverbs and funny stories from his childhood, though I've wondered more than once if he doesn't make up half of them. The stories anyway."

"And the proverbs?"

"Let see…one of his favorites is 'count your nights by stars, not shadows, count your life with smiles, not tears.'"

"And your favorite?"

"My favorite?" A slight blush crept across her face. "'In the middle of life, love enters and makes it a fairy tale.'"

"I can see why Thomas fell in love with you. Especially with Italy in the background.

"I'm sorry," he said, when she didn't respond. "That was too personal."

"No…" She looked up at him. "It's fine. I let

Thomas go a long time ago, but that doesn't mean it's been easy to relive it all."

He knew she still felt the sting of betrayal. He wished he could take that part of her memories away. Because he hadn't expected to care so much. But there was something about Talia, with her passion for life, that had him dreading the moment when they found the paintings and she didn't need him anymore. When his life went back to normal. If he could call anything about his life normal.

"You ready to go?"

"Just about." He glanced at his watch. "Have you heard back yet from your brother-in-law?"

Talia shook her head. "Not yet, but I'll try again."

"No answer?" he asked after she set the phone down.

She shook her head. "I'm just being paranoid again. He probably got called into work an extra shift."

But she didn't have to say anything for him to know that she was worried. Whoever was behind this had made a handful of threats. And if they were threatening her sister, why not Marco, as well?

"It's still pretty early," he said. "Maybe he's still asleep."

"Maybe." But she didn't look convinced.

"What does he do for a living?" he asked.

"He delivers cargo to restaurants and shops. All of it's done by boat, of course."

He dropped his napkin onto his plate. They needed to find her brother-in-law, get into the apartment and find those paintings.

Ten minutes later, they were making their way across one of the bridges down the narrow street. He'd seen photos of the city, but like with his first impression of the canal, in person the colors seemed even brighter. Apartment buildings with flower boxes and shutters had been painted in oranges, yellows and browns. Below them the water sparkled in the morning sunlight, while boats made their way down the narrower veins of the canals.

One day he really would like to find the time to visit this country while he wasn't chasing down the bad guys. And from what he knew about her, no doubt Talia would be the perfect tour guide. He'd love to see the city, not as a tourist per se, but through the eyes of a local.

"How far's the apartment?" he asked.

"Just a couple more minutes. It's in a more private, less touristy neighborhood."

He watched one of the gondoliers propel his black, flat-bottomed boat across the water with a yellow rowing oar. "Have you ever taken one of those?"

"Never have. Can you believe that?"

"Too touristy?"

"Thomas's family has their own boat. Didn't make sense to pay for a thirty-minute ride through the canals when he could take me for free."

There was something peaceful about this city. Completely different from where he came from, where cars filled the street, and pedestrians had to fight for the right away.

"I think my father-in-law would have moved away years ago if it was up to him, but Thomas's mother...I don't think she'll ever leave the house, or Italy, for that matter. She insists that modern cities destroy the sense of community."

He didn't blame her. Stone paving lined the narrow streets. Supplies were being transported along the water, as goods were delivered to the local bakeries, pastry shops, and grocers. Bright yellow one a row of apartments had faded, its plaster chipping off the walls that were lined with green shutters and flower boxes sitting on tiny window sills. Laundry fluttered in the wind above them as they walked across another bridge. There was a sense of community in the small shops and houses away from the busy tourist sections.

"Personally I think it would be hard to leave a timeless place like this," he said.

Talia pulled out her phone and called him again.

"I'm still not getting him," she said, after letting it ring a dozen times. "Let me see if their neighbor has a key."

A minute later, Joe could sense the unease in Talia's body language as she returned with a neighbor, a woman in her late fifties. The neighbor nodded at him, then slid the key into the door of the apartment.

The tour of Venice was over.

"Hello?" She flipped on the overhead light in the darkened room.

He stepped into the quiet apartment behind her and looked around the living room. "Doesn't look like anyone's here."

She heard her suck in a lungful of air.

"Talia?"

He rushed over to where she was standing. A body lay on the floor next to the dining room table. Blood pooled beneath his head. His open eyes were lifeless.

The neighbor screamed.

"No. No...this can't be possible." Talia pressed her hand against her mouth and shook her head. "It's Marco."

TWELVE

Talia she couldn't stop staring at Marco's lifeless body. She felt numb. Frozen. This had to be yet another bad dream. But instead it was a waking nightmare that refused to end.

Signora Nicolai, who'd been a neighbor of the family for decades, grabbed her arm, her face turning to a chalky gray.

"I just spoke to him a couple days ago," the older woman said in Italian, her breathing suddenly labored. "He'd come by to water his mother's plants and check on things. Told me he'd come back today and hang up a new mirror I just bought. He was such a nice young man."

Talia glanced up at Joe. "Are you sure he's dead?"

Joe kneeled down by the body to feel for a pulse, then looked back up at the two of them. "I'm sorry. He's gone. Ask her if she heard anything. A gunshot? People shouting? Anything."

Talia quickly translated the questions into Italian.

"No, I didn't hear anything," the older woman said. "We need to call the police."

Talia nodded. "Why don't you go call them now? We'll wait here with the body."

She turned back as the woman hurried away, the soles of her shoes clicking against the sidewalk. It was strange the things that she noticed. The buzz of the overhead light. A fly landing on the coffee table. The slightly musty smell from having the house closed up in the heat.

All in an attempt to avoid what was right in front of them.

The only reason she was alive was because Anna thought she still needed her. But if she couldn't find the paintings, or if she discovered Talia had recognized her, it was going to be her body lying dead on the ground somewhere.

Like Marco.

Like Thomas.

She walked over to Marco's body, stopping a few feet from him. This was no accident. Blood had pooled on the floor beneath him from a gunshot to the head. How long had he been there before he'd died? Alone? No one should have to die that way.

A surge of anger shot through her as she fought back the tears. Anna had gotten to him. But why? Marco had nothing to do with any of this. She leaned against the back of the leather couch to steady herself. Her legs and hands were shaking. Her mind was spinning with implications…

Her mind flashed back to Thomas's death. She'd sat in the interrogation room and they'd shown her photos of his body at the crime scene as they'd tried to determine if she was connected to his crimes. The photos would always be imprinted on her mind.

"Talia?" Joe stepped between her and the body and pressed his hands against her arms. "Take a deep breath. I know this is hard."

She took a step back.

"It looks as if Marco walked in on her," Joe stated.

Talia glanced up at the tall ceiling, the large chandelier hanging in the center and the familiar blue walls. She noticed now what Joe was seeing. The living room had been searched. She could tell from the photos hanging askew on the wall. From the way her father-in-law's books lay strewn on the floor. And how the narrow rows of white shelves going up the wall with dozens of knickknacks and photos were a jumbled mess.

Anna had been here, looking for the paintings, and somehow Marco had gotten in the way.

"So what do you think happened?" she asked. "Anna was searching the house when Marco arrived. She panics and shoots him?"

"Makes sense." He nodded at a broken lamp. "There was definitely a struggle."

"He tried to fight back."

"And she shot him," Joe said.

"Someone had to have heard something," she said.

Joe was walking around the room, systematically studying the scene. "But if the shooter knows anything about guns—like Anna would—and if she used a suppressor, it would change the sound enough that it might not be recognized."

"Once the police arrive, they're going to start asking a slew of questions, and we still haven't found the paintings," she said. "Even if they are here in the apartment, we won't be able to search for them."

She felt the heat of the space press against her chest. "How much time do you think we have until the police get here?" he asked. "Five...ten minutes?"

"At the most."

"Then we need to work fast. Because you're right. Once they get here, they're going to block off the house and won't let us look, but if we can find the paintings—assuming she didn't find them—before the police turn up, we might be able to end all of this before someone else is hurt."

Talia looked around the trashed living space of her mother-in-law's normally perfectly clean house. "And if the paintings have already been found?"

"Until we know otherwise, let's assume they haven't at this point."

She was staring at the body again, remembering Marco's karaoke attempts at the annual family gathering. His insisting that his mom make his grandmother's recipe for homemade cannelloni stuffed with veal, pork, ricotta and parmigiano. Her breath caught. And she remembered Thomas lying just as still in a wooden casket at his funeral. The brothers had looked so much alike, with their dark hair, tan skin and lighter eyes. This never should have happened. If she hadn't come here in the first place—

"Talia, I know this is hard, but you need to stay with me," Joe said, stepping back in front of her. "We don't have a lot of time."

She drew in a deep breath and tried to focus. She could do this. She'd deal with Marco's death later, but for now, Joe was right. If the paintings were still here, they needed to find them.

"Do you know where his mother kept Thomas's things?"

"There's a trunk in the guest room. It seems like the most logical place to start."

"Go see if there's anything still there, and I'll see what I can find in here."

Talia moved quickly through the familiar apartment. The police would see it initially as a home invasion gone wrong, but she knew better. And knew how Marco's parents' lives would never be the same again. Surprisingly, the guest bedroom looked untouched. Apparently Marco's arrival might have gotten him killed, but it seemed like it also had scared their burglar into fleeing.

Inside the guest room, she glanced at the brushed orange wallpaper and solid wood furniture. The trunk sat at the end of the bed. She pushed away the memories of staying here with Thomas and concentrated instead on finding the paintings.

Her heart raced as she searched. Any second now she'd hear the sirens. She lifted the lid of the trunk and breathed in the musty smell of mothballs. She found a leather box with Thomas's name written on the outside. Talia took in a deep breath before opening it up. Inside was the watch she'd given him for his thirtieth birthday. Postcards he'd sent her and his parents. Birthday and anniversary cards. A couple ball caps he used to wear. His class ring...

All things she hadn't been able to look at after his death.

She kept going through things until she got to the bottom of the box.

But there were no paintings.

She looked around the room, then decided to pull open the door of the armoire next to the window. Inside were coats and a pile of winter blankets.

I don't know what to do, God. I don't know how to end this.

She pulled open a dresser drawer and started rummaging through neatly folded towels and tablecloths. After Thomas's death she'd found herself in a downward spiral. Faced with not only his death, but also his guilt, she'd blamed

God for what had happened. Slowly things had changed. She'd realized that Thomas's guilt didn't change who God was. He was still God.

Death was never a part of God's original plan.

Joe's words ran through her mind again. Living in a fallen world had brought the grief and pain and death. And despite all that had happened today, God's faithfulness was just as real after a tragedy as it had been before. Even when it seemed impossible to see. It was what she had to hold on to when the countless doubts began to surface.

Joe made a quick sweep of the room. It was clear someone had been searching for something. What wasn't clear was if they'd found what they were after. The clock on the wall clicked down the seconds, a steady, rhythmic beat, reminding him that they only had a few minutes—if that—to find what they were looking for.

He crouched down on the large rug in the center of the living room and glanced under one of the couches. A cell phone had slid under the edge. He pulled it out, clicked it on, then swiped the unlock.

Bingo. Unlocked.

It was amazing to him how many people didn't use any kind of lock for their screen, but not locking the phone was common. The background photo was of Marco and a dark-haired woman. He glanced at the body a few feet from him, then checked the call log. Nothing stood out. Next he ran through the emails and wished he knew Italian. He stopped at one sent the previous day with three attached photos.

Joe clicked on the attachments. One by one they popped up. They were photos of the three paintings. The paintings they were looking for. Which meant Marco's parents had to have told him about them. He ran through one of the probable scenarios in his mind. Marco's parents called to tell him Talia was coming for some of Thomas's possessions. He'd looked for them and found them. Maybe he'd been curious about why she wanted them. Or perhaps suspicious as to why she would suddenly want a look at some of Thomas's possessions. They knew what their son had been involved in. Did they think she knew what he'd been doing?

He glanced at the message in the email. He might not speak Italian, but he could figure out a couple of the words. The email address was to a gallery. Marco had been asking someone for the value of the paintings. Which meant he tried to find out how much they were worth.

He glanced at the clock on the wall. Three minutes had passed.

"Talia?" Joe hurried to the doorway of the bedroom, where she was going through a trunk. "We're running out of time. I figure we've only got a couple more minutes before the police show up, but I think I've found something."

"Good," she said, stepping back from the trunk. "Because I've gone through everything, and the paintings aren't here."

"That's because Marco already found them." He held up the cell phone and showed her one of the photos. "He sent an email with photos of the paintings attached to a gallery."

She moved beside him and shook her head. "I never told him specifically what we were coming here for."

"Maybe your in-laws told him because he took pictures of the paintings and sent them to someone for an appraisal."

"Who did he send them to?"

Joe glanced at the email. "The address says Sienna Gallery. Do you know where that is?"

"It's an art gallery here in Venice on the other side of the island."

"There's also a response," he said, handing her the phone to translate the Italian.

"Looks like he received a response from a Signor De Luca, who told him he would need to look at the paintings in person in order to do any real evaluation of their worth." She looked up at Joe. "He didn't trust me."

"You don't know that."

"I know that if he'd never come here looking for them, he might be alive today."

"You can't be sure of that, either." He instantly regretted the sharpness in his tone, but neither of them needed to be playing guessing games on what might have happened. "It doesn't matter what Marco was thinking at this point. We need to go talk to this signore. See if there was any further conversation between them. See if he went ahead and took them in to be appraised in person."

She glanced toward the front door. "But what about the police?"

"If we stay, they're going to detain us for questioning. We can always come back later and answer their questions."

He could hear the sirens from the police boats in the background. Time was running out.

She nodded.

Five minutes later, he was following her onto the crowded floating jetty of the public ferry, the quickest way, she'd told him, to get to the gallery. He rested his hand against the small of her back as they pressed onto the *vaporetto,* ensuring they got a spot near the exit in case he decided they needed to get off at one of the stops in a hurry.

The boat moved away from the platform, then made its way down the canal, past rows of docks. He could see the green dome of a building in the distance. Birds dove under a bridge as they passed under the structure. Tourists flooded the walkways, their thoughts on nothing more than experiencing first hand St. Mark's Square, an iconic gondola ride down the Grand Canal and a plate of fresh pasta.

He shifted his attention to the passengers on the boat, and to each person on every subsequent platform they stopped at. Because if Anna was here, he was going to find her.

"It's beautiful, isn't it? The river. The buildings," Talia said, breaking the silence between them. "All this beauty, and yet all I can think about is Marco."

He glanced down at her, realizing she hadn't had time to grieve, let alone process what she'd just seen. And for her, this case had just become even more personal. She might not be married to Thomas anymore, but he'd sensed the affection she still had for his family despite any tension still lingering between them. She was the kind of person who loved intensely. Which meant a situation like this had to continuously drag up places in the past she'd probably prefer to leave undisturbed.

"Do you think we should have stayed?" she asked.

"I think we have to first find a way to make sense of all of this. Marco's death. Thomas's death. My brother's death. Staying would have simply delayed that process."

"You know this is my fault," she said. "Marco's death."

"Talia, stop right there. I meant what I said earlier. That's a place you can't go, because none of this is your fault."

"But it is." She looked up at him. "I knew they would figure out we were coming here, and that they didn't trust me to deliver the paintings. They had to make sure they got here first. And now Marco is dead because he somehow got involved. He probably had no idea what he getting into when he found those paintings and started asking how much they were worth."

"All of that might be true, but his death is still not your fault."

"How am I going tell his parents?" The wind blew against her hair, blowing strands across her face. She pushed them away. "This has to stop."

He took her hand, wishing he *could* make all of this go away for her. Wishing he could take her back to the day before all of this happened. But they could only move forward through this together. "The local Italian police have the photo of Anna and are looking for her."

"And if that's not enough? That wasn't enough for Marco. If she manages to get to my sister or me, or—"

"Don't go there, Talia."

He wished he could tell her that all of this was going to have a happy ending. Except he knew he couldn't. Not when someone out there was bent on destruction.

He stared out across the water. The breeze from the water was the only thing relieving the heavy humidity hanging in the air. What if there was nothing he could do?

She squeezed his hand, then nodded as the boat approached the next floating jetty. "This is our stop. The shop's just a couple minutes off the beaten path."

Talia led them quickly away from the water, down a maze of narrow passageways lined with heavy wooden doors. He was going to need to call his boss and tell him what was going on, but he was worried that once he did, he'd be pulled off the case. Which was why for the moment it was better to figure things out on his own.

THIRTEEN

They stepped into the shop filled with dozens of sculptures on display and art hanging on the walls. As an artist, it was a place where she could easily spend days getting lost in the artwork. But at the moment she needed to focus.

"Buongiorno," Talia said to the man behind the counter in Italian before switching to English for Joe's benefit. "I need to speak to Signor De Luca."

"I'm sorry, but that isn't possible right now. Signor De Luca is on the phone with a client."

She tapped her fingers against the counter. Time was running out and she wasn't in the mood for delays.

Beside her, Joe pulled out his badge, clearly feeling the same urgency she was. "I'm Agent Bryant with the FBI's art crime team. It's extremely important that we ask your boss a few questions immediately."

The man glanced at the badge and nodded. "Of course. I'm sure he will be happy to help the FBI. If you'll just give me a moment."

"I should get me one of those badges," Talia said, as the man slipped through a door into the back. "But in the meantime, you're not a bad person to have on someone's side when in a jam."

"Ha." Joe let out a low laugh. "I was hoping you wouldn't mind my direct approach, but it's a method that works. Besides, I figure we don't have time to mess around with formalities or Signor De Luca's timetable."

A minute later an older Italian gentleman with gray hair along his temples stepped up behind the counter. Even in the July heat he wore a button-down shirt and jacket.

Talia stepped forward and laid her hands on the counter. "Signor De Luca, my name is Talia Morello. I was married to Thomas Morello before his death three years ago."

The older man frowned. "I'm acquainted with your family, and sorry for your loss. But I'm not sure what that has to do with the FBI?"

She motioned to Joe. "This is Agent Joe Bryant. He works with the FBI's art crime team."

"How can I help you?"

Joe glanced at Signor De Luca's colleague. "Could we speak in private?"

"Of course. Why don't you follow me to my office."

A moment later they were standing in a cluttered office filled with an overflow of artwork, piles of papers and books and a clearly antiquated filing system.

"I understand that Thomas's brother, Marco, sent you some photographs of some paintings to appraise," Talia said, once the older man had closed the door behind them.

"He asked me if they might be worth any money."

"And what did you tell him?"

The older Italian hesitated. "I'm sorry, but I'm afraid that any business I do with potential clients is all confidential, including quotes. And I'm still not sure why you're asking these questions."

"We're asking these questions," she countered, "because people have already died because of those paintings."

"Died…? I had no idea. I told him that I'd have to see them in person for me to be sure, but if they were real, which they appeared to be from the photo, they were some of Li Fonti's original paintings and would be worth several million to the right buyer. He said he was going to bring them in this morning, but I haven't seen him yet."

Because he's dead.

And she wasn't ready to tell him that.

"Are you okay?" Signor De Luca studied Talia's expression. "What's really going on?"

"All I can say at this point," Joe said, "is that some very bad people want to get their hands on those paintings. And they are willing to do whatever it takes to get them."

"I wish I could help you, but you know as much as I do. Without seeing the paintings in person I can't be positive, but that's exactly what I told Marco."

Talia glanced at Joe. There was nothing more they could do here.

"Thank you for speaking with us, Signor De Luca."

"You're welcome, and if you do happen to get your hands on those paintings, I would love to look at them."

"What was your relationship with Marco and his parents, especially after Thomas's death?" Joe asked Talia, once they were outside the gallery and heading back toward the *vaporetto*.

Talia hurried to keep up with him. "What do you mean?"

"Did they blame you at all? Think you were anyway involved in the money he'd been stealing from the apartment?"

She slowed her pace. Small beads of moisture dotted the back of her neck from the rising temperature. She wanted him to ask her if she'd take him on a tour of the city, a romantic boat ride through the canals, or where to buy the best fresh pasta... Anything but this line of questioning.

She swallowed hard. "You mean do they still wonder if I wasn't involved with what Thomas did? And that I'm showing up now to claim what's 'mine' so I can cash in?"

"I know that's a tough question, but yes. I think we need to consider everything."

She bit the inside of her lip. "I don't think so. I can't say that we're extremely close, especially after Thomas's death, but his family has always been extremely supportive of me. But here's another thing." She stopped on the bridge they were crossing and grasped the wrought-iron railing. "It's still possible that Anna has the paintings."

"I agree, and if she does, she's not going to hang around here. She'll have an exit plan to leave the country, sell them and disappear. Unfortunately at this point there's no way for us to know for sure."

"So what do we do now?" she asked. "I feel like we're at another dead end."

"We need to find Anna."

She stared out across the narrow waterway. A boat bobbed in the water that hovered just beneath doorways. She knew he was right, but while part of her wanted to find both the paintings and Anna, the other part of her just wanted to run.

"I never should have brought you with me," he said, clearly sensing her hesitation. "I thought it would make things easier to find the paintings, but now I'm worried that I've put your life in more danger by bringing you here."

"You're the one who was shot." She grasped on to his good arm with her fingertips, then pulled away. "I need to see this through as well, because just like you this is personal. It's affecting people I care about. I might want to walk away, but I can't."

"I just want—need—to keep you safe."

But even he couldn't guarantee he could keep her safe.

Her hands trembled and her legs felt weak.

Between the heat and the shock of seeing Marco's body, she felt completely rattled.

Joe brushed a strand of hair out of her face then took her hands. "Your face is pale and your hands are clammy." He squeezed her hands, then let them go. "Sit down. I'll go buy you something to drink."

"I really will be okay, Joe. I'm just shaken. We need to get back to the boat and go talk to the police."

She started walking again, and tried to ignore the strong pull of emotions swirling through her, and the heat pounding down on her.

"I'm serious, Talia. There's a bench up ahead and a place where we can get some water," he said. "You sit down, and I'll buy us both something cold to drink."

"I wasn't even the one who was shot."

"Don't worry about me." He shot her a smile. "I've always been tough as nails."

They walked into the large, open square. She obeyed and sat down at one of the benches while Joe went to get the drinks, close enough to where he could still see her. Even at this time of day, the square was already filling up with tourists. Cafés were setting up their outside tables for the lunch rush with tablecloths and flowers on each table.

A woman sat down next to her.

Talia started to stand up, then stopped when she saw the gun.

Anna.

Her chest started pressing against her lungs. "What do you want from me, Anna?"

"I thought you might recognize me. And at this point, I'm pretty sure you know exactly what I want. In the meantime, though, I'm going to need you to come with me."

"Forget it."

She glanced at the gun and frowned. "I'd really hate to have to shoot you, but trust me, I will. It's not like I have anything to lose."

"You wouldn't shoot me. Not with dozens of potential witnesses out there."

"Do you really want to test me? I can be lost in this crowd in a matter of seconds. Which means you scream or try to get someone's attention, and I'll not only shoot you, but one of these nice tourists in this crowd. Or maybe I'll take a shot at Joe again, and I can promise you, I won't miss this time."

She could see the intensity in Anna's eyes. She had nothing to lose and everything to gain.

How had she gone from wanting to save people to this?

Talia looked back at Joe, who was paying the cashier. "Where are we going?"

"Does it matter? You think your hero's going to come to your rescue, don't you? But I've ensured that he's going to be tied up for a few more minutes."

Talia felt the knot in her stomach tighten. Anna had everything planed. A backup for anything that went wrong. But she was also desperate. Which gave Talia an advantage. She just had to find a way to play at Anna's weakness.

"Let's go." Anna gripped Talia's arm. "Now."

Joe collected his change from the vender along with the two waters, then turned around and bumped into a woman holding a baby in the process. The woman's bag dropped to the ground between them.

"*Mi perdoni*...I'm sorry."

"No. It was my fault." He shoved his change into his pocket, then picked up the bag and handed it back to her. He turned to where Talia had been sitting only seconds before.

She was gone.

He dropped the water bottles and started

running toward the bench where he'd left her. His heart pounded in his chest as panic set in. How had this happened? She'd been there one moment and the next she'd vanished...

He kept running, ignoring the pain radiating through his arm with each jolting step on the stone walkway. He saw a motorized boat disappearing around the corner of the building. There were dozens of narrow streets and canals crisscrossing their way through the city and he had no idea which way she'd gone.

His phone rang in his pocket. He paused, then answered the unknown number.

"Mr. Bryant. It's nice to finally talk in person."

"Anna Hayes." His stomach clenched. "Where's Talia?"

"She's safe. For now. But don't even bother to try and find us."

"Just tell me where you are—where Talia is—and end this before someone else gets hurt. We know about Marco, and the local police have your name and description—"

"Your attempts to threaten and intimidate me won't work. I tried to warn you, but neither of you would listen. It was supposed to be so simple. She was supposed to bring me the paintings, and I was going to disappear."

"Just let Talia go."

Joe blew out a sharp breath. He had a feeling the woman couldn't be reasoned with. And what had Talia had told her? Did she know they hadn't found the artwork yet?

Whatever the case, this was a game that needed to end.

"I want you to listen very carefully to me," Anna continued. "I realize now that I went to the wrong person looking for the paintings."

"So what is she? A hostage?"

"For the moment. And here's what you're going to do. Take a flight to Rome, where you're going to get on the next plane back to the US."

He kept walking, praying he'd catch sight of them. They couldn't be that far ahead. Her planned distraction had only lasted a few seconds. But which direction? "You think I'm just going to walk away from her, or even if I do, that the police won't find you?"

"You will do exactly what I'm saying, unless you want her dead, as well."

"What's going to stop you from killing her no matter what I do?"

He tried to mask the desperation in his voice as he kept walking. She had to be out somewhere. Inside an apartment or a shop or lost in a sea of tourists. On the water in one of the boats…

"Let me speak with her before I do anything."

"Call me from the airport in Rome, and I'll let you speak to her. And don't try my patience. You know what happens when you do."

The call ended.

The waterfront was bustling with tourists taking photos and selfies. There were hundreds of streets, several hundred canals and even more houses and places of business. All of which made hiding from the police—at least temporarily—possible.

Or for all he knew they could be leaving the island now.

Except Anna wasn't going to do that. Not if she still believed the paintings to still be here. She might not have found what Marco did with them, but she'd stay on the island, and use Talia as her leverage. Which meant she wasn't going anywhere. And neither was he.

Joe's phone rang again.

"Esposito," he said. "Tell me you've got something, because we've got a problem."

"I was just checking in with you. What's wrong?"

"Anna Hayes's got Talia. She's trying to use her now as leverage to get those paintings."

"Where do you think she's headed?"

"I don't think she'll leave the island until she has what she wants. But I also believe she's running on adrenaline and not thinking clearly. She's taking too many chances. She'd told me to leave the country, or she'll kill Talia."

"I'll make sure the local police have photos of both women. She's not going to get away with this. Because if she's here, we'll find her."

"Keep me updated."

Joe ended the call then put in one of his own to the States. If Anna still had her phone on her, he might have just found a way track her.

A minute later he was connected to a secure FBI line. "This is Agent Joe Bryant. I need a call traced that just came into my phone."

"Okay, but that's going to take a few minutes," a woman said.

"I don't have time. A woman has been kidnapped, and her life's in danger."

"I understand, but I'll need to put you on hold while I trace the call."

He could feel the seconds ticking. The Grand Canal lapped alongside the buildings. Boats left a trail of white behind them. A man jumped into a boat next to a line of colorful mooring poles, then pulled at the motor before joining the flow of traffic in the canal. A couple floated past on a gondola. Customers sipped at their coffee and stared out across the water.

But he had no idea where Talia was.

"You still there?"

"I'm still here," he said. "What have you got?"

"I found her. She's moving away from your position on the south side of the island."

Where was she going?

His mind battled for the best option, but as far as he was concerned, he only had one. "I need you to take me to her. Pull up a map of the city and take me on the most direct route."

"That's not going to be easy." He caught the hesitation in her voice.

"Is it doable?"

"Yeah…I think so."

"Then get me to her. I don't think she'll leave the island. Not yet anyway."

"Okay. I've got a map in front of me with your location as well as her cell phone GPS pinpointed on the map."

Joe stood in the middle of a lake of tourists. Life went on. No one had any idea what was going on. "Which way do I go?"

"Head west…left. There's a narrow alley-way just ahead of you. When you get to it, turn right."

He moved out at a fast pace, weaving his way through the tourists who were enthralled with the offerings at the shops. Venetian carnival masks, hand-blown glass filling up the windows.

"Take a left at the next T junction."

"Do you still have her?"

"She's still moving down one of the canals. I'll let you know if she stops."

A minute later, he was moving away from the mobs of tourists to the quieter streets. He hoped he was making the right decision and wasn't off on another wild-goose chase. It seemed that Anna didn't know he might have the capability to follow her. But if she was rattled and her plan began to fall apart, she was going to make mistakes. What he couldn't have happen was for Talia to get caught up in the crossfire.

"Talk to me," he said, moving at a slow jog.

"Keep going another hundred yards, then take a left."

He stared down the long empty alley. "Are you sure?"

"Yes…go. It's a shortcut."

Pipes and electrical wires competed for space with ivy up the brick walls. If he put his hands out he'd be able to touch both sides of the wall. There were private houses and graffiti on the walls. Locked doors, brick walls, barred windows, elaborate doors, opening up to wider, stone pavement. The farther he got from the tourist district the quieter the streets became. Local residents walked the narrow streets carrying shopping bags. Schoolchildren ran through the street.

He came to another canal.

"Turn left again and go over the bridge."

He could smell garlic and onions coming from a small pizzeria, as he passed a dock with a row of boats bobbing in the water. Colorful wooden posts jetted up from the water. Bells rang in the background from one of the churches…

"Where is she?"

"Give me a second."

Don't let me lose her now, God, please. Not now.

"You're close. One street over and another fifty feet."

"Is she on a boat?"

"Maybe. I'm not sure."

He started running. Tracking her down in the water was going to be even more difficult.

"Wait a minute…looks like another twenty feet and you should see her."

But he couldn't.

The canal flowed beside him, and he could see at least half a dozen boats. He searched for Talia's red shirt. Nothing.

Where are you, Talia?

FOURTEEN

Talia felt the butt of the gun press against her lower back and the grip of Anna's fingers pressing tightly around her arm as they weaved through the almost deserted streets. As soon as they'd left the piazza, Anna had immediately steered them away from the heavy pedestrian traffic that ran through the popular sections of Venice like St. Mark's Square and the route to the Rialto. Away from those tourist hot spots you could find quieter streets, where one could almost forget that twenty-five million people visited the island each year.

She'd discovered it was like that in almost every heavily trafficked tourist town. Most of the crowds tended to stick to the main arteries of the city and the tourist traps, when only a few minutes away you could find the underlying beauty and culture of a place that most people missed.

But she wasn't here this time as a tour guide.

Instead she was here fighting for her life.

She glanced behind her, down the empty street. Joe would have noticed she was gone by now, but finding her in this maze of streets, canals and foot bridges was going to be difficult, if not impossible.

Talia stumbled over a lose brick in the pavement. Anna's grip tightened as they turned quickly down yet another quiet street.

"Hurry up," Anna said. "We don't exactly have all day."

"So what happens next?"

"Like I told your FBI hero, I went to the wrong person for the paintings. I should have gone directly to your in-laws. And since there's a good chance they're going to need some motivation to hand them over, having you will help guarantee that they do what they are told."

Talia winced at Anna's tightening grip around her arm. "They've already lost two sons—"

"Trying to get me to feel sorry for them isn't going to work. You of all people should know that by now."

An older gentleman stepped out of one of the buildings, locked a heavy wooden door with a key, then started walking toward them at a leisurely pace. Talia's jaw clenched. This had already gone too far. If she didn't take a chance and do something—

"Remember what I said." Anna's words broke into her thoughts. "I can't have you going and making a scene, now can I, Talia? I'd hate to have to shoot the man, but I will."

Fear encircled like a tangible presence. What was going to happen if she didn't get away, or if Joe didn't find her? Anna clearly didn't have a problem with eliminating people. Once she got what she wanted, Anna would end up killing her and disposing of her body somewhere out in the surrounding islands or out in the sea.

Talia drew in a deep breath of humid air. But Anna wasn't going to get her way. Not this time. Because she wasn't going down that road again without a fight. But neither could she put the life of someone else at risk. The man walked past them, completely unaware of the situation. She was going to have to find a way to escape without putting anyone's life in danger. Which meant she needed to get away from Anna.

She kept walking while her mind fought for a solution, but the odds weren't exactly in her favor. She might have taken a number of self-defense classes over the years, but Anna had been trained by law enforcement. And in order to escape, she was going to have to take down Anna.

Her shoes clipped against the brick-lined street that was empty again. Music played from one of the apartments above. Someone was cooking. They couldn't be far from one of the arteries of the canal, where there would be boats and maybe someone who could help her. She glanced back at Anna. The woman might be better trained, but she'd also relaxed her grip on her arm and no longer had her gun pointed at her. There was another street twenty feet or so up ahead and to the right. She wasn't sure where it went, but gut instinct told her if she was going to run it needed to be now.

Turning quickly, she thrust her elbow into Anna's throat while at the same time pitching her weight forward to give her the leverage she needed. Anna stumbled backward, then groaned as she slammed into the brick wall. Talia didn't waste any time as she ran for the adjacent alley, then made the sharp turn to the right down another narrow street, with apartments towering over her. If she could get far enough ahead of Anna in the maze of streets, she just might be able to lose her.

She reached the end of the street and made

another turn. Humidity hung heavy around her, making it hard to breath. She kept moving forward, unwilling to risk slowing down just to look back. Because she knew Anna was somewhere behind her. She took another corner and looked for the canal. She needed to find Joe. Needed to find someone who could get her out of here without getting either of them shot.

A bullet pinged off the brick wall next to her. Talia ducked into an alcove with a large wooden door, her heart racing. She tried the handle, her chest heaving, but it was locked. She was out of options. It was another fifty feet or so until the next street, and Anna was closing in behind her. She'd never make it.

"You don't learn, do you?" Anna stopped in front of her, gun pointed directly at Talia's heart. "Or maybe you don't believe I'm serious. But you need to listen to me very carefully. That shot—that was a warning. You know I can hit any target. Like your FBI friend. That shot was calculated. But next time I won't be aiming for the wall behind you. Or your friend's arm."

Talia shivered despite the heat as Anna pulled a zip tie cord from her back pocket and quickly secured her hands behind her. "I had hoped I wouldn't have to do this. It's hard to look like two happy tourists on a stroll when one of them is tied up, but we don't have much farther to go, and I'm not to take another chance of your doing something stupid. Now let's go."

Talia winced as Anna grabbed her by the arm and started back down the street.

I can't do this on my own, God. I've tried. And I don't want anyone else getting hurt, but I need a way out...

Anna turned another corner then walked across a footbridge that spanned the murky canal water. There was a boat on the other side of the quiet space, bobbing in the water.

"Come on." Anna caught her gaze. "And don't try something stupid."

Talia glanced back, still praying that Joe would find her. But if they left the main island, the odds of him finding her were only going to decrease dramatically.

"Where are we going?" she asked.

"It doesn't matter." Anna jumped onto the boat, pulling Talia onboard behind her. "Sit down under the awning and be quiet."

She started the engine, then quickly maneuvered down the narrow waterway. Talia felt her options of escape evaporating. Her chances of jumping overboard and making it to shore were slim to none unless she could get her hands untied. And if she called out for help... Anna had already made herself clear on that one. On top of that, she was partially hidden beneath the canopy, which would make it harder for her to signal someone.

"You seem to know Venice better than I would have thought," Talia said. Until she could figure out a way to escape, she might as well try to get some answers.

"I backpacked across Italy one summer during college and Venice was one of the stops we made. I did have to spend some time studying a map once I discovered you were coming here. And to be honest, even a map doesn't truly show how complicated the six main neighborhoods and street layout of Venice are. I thought about relying on a local, but even you know how far that got me the last time. It's always better to do things yourself if you want things done."

"Even with the risk of getting caught?"

"If you think I can't make it through the canals, you're wrong. I grew up near the Mississippi gulf coast. The Grand Bay is a maze of bayous, bays and marsh islands. My brother and I used to take out a skiff during summer vacation and explore the area. I've never really liked being in the water, but I loved driving the boat. And while Venice might be a bit more well-known than my hometown, I've found that I feel right at home here."

They were heading out of the canal. If they made it out to the open water…

"Do you really think this is going to have a happy ending for you?" Talia asked.

Anna laughed. "A couple million seems like pretty good to me."

"Not if you have to spend your time watching your back."

"Who said I was going to be on the run? There are dozens of places I can disappear to. I looked into Thailand, for example. The weather is perfect most of the year, and the cost of living is cheap. There's plenty of western-style restaurants and entertainment if I get bored. Do you know how far that much money could go in a place like that?"

"And you think that just because you live overseas the FBI will drop the case?" Talia asked.

"Just like you think your FBI hero won't stop looking for you?" Anna turned around and frowned. "You know, I'm really tired of listening to your questions."

Anna swung the gun across Talia's temple. Lights exploded behind her eyes, then everything went dark.

Joe kept running down the canal, searching for a glimpse of Talia. He had no doubt about who was behind this. No doubt as well that the woman with the baby had been a plant to distract him. All it had taken was seconds for Talia to disappear. Why hadn't he just stayed with her?

"Joe, are you still there?"

"Yes, I'm here." The phone cracked. He couldn't lose the connection. "Can you hear me?"

"Okay, you're back. It looks like the boat's leaving the canal and heading out into the open water. Which means we've got a problem. You won't be able to follow on foot."

Where was she going?

He might not be a tour guide, but he did know there were over a hundred islands that made up Venice, as well as the mainland. It would be possible for her to leave the main island and hide out somewhere else. Close enough to return when needed, and yet remote enough to avoid detection.

"Wait a minute…I think I spotted her."

"Are you sure?"

"Yeah." He could see someone in a red shirt sitting beneath the awning of a boat. The woman at the wheel matched Anna's description. It had to be them.

"If you can get access to a boat I might be able to help you follow her."

"Okay."

"Wait a minute…"

"What's wrong?"

"The signal just went dead."

"Meaning?"

"I don't know. She must have dumped the phone or taken out the battery."

I need something else, God. Please…I can't lose her now.

Joe expelled a sharp breath as he ran down the sidewalk along the water, while keeping his eye on the boat that was now heading out of the canal. A young man in his early twenties was working in the back of a cargo boat organizing supplies on the small transport vessel.

"I need a ride," Joe shouted, searching for the Italian words as he approached the boat. "A—a *barca. Rapido.*"

"I speak English," the other man said in a thick accent. "What is the problem?"

"I'm with the FBI." Joe pulled out his badge and stepped onto the boat. "A woman's just been kidnapped."

The man hesitated, studying the badge. "And you're with the FBI?"

"Yes. I need to catch up with that boat. Please."

"Get in." The man nodded, then switched on the outboard motor as Joe pointed in the direction the other boat had gone. "I always wanted to join my country's secret service and become an agent. All the action, covert ops, shootouts with the bad guys, women..."

Joe frowned, wishing he'd hurry. "Not everything you see on television is true."

The reality was that ninety percent of what he did revolved around paperwork, not chasing bad guys and getting in shootouts. Though those statistics had just been shattered over the past few of days. He'd been shot, and now someone he'd promised to protect had just been taken from him.

"Can you hurry? Please. Around that next corner. They're getting away."

"Which boat was she in?"

"The small, flat-bottomed boat with the white awning. Six or seven meters long with an outboard motor."

"We call those a *topetta*. You can rent them, and even maneuver the lagoons without a guide, which might be smart if you wanted to go undetected."

"There it is."

"I see it, and I'm going as fast as I can, but the traffic's pretty controlled. There actually are speed limits out here."

Joe stared straight ahead, keeping his focus on the boat they were following. Since they weren't going to be able to track it via GPS, they were going to have to make sure they didn't lose it.

"What happened to your arm?" the man said.

Joe looked down at his wound. The man asked too many questions. But a patch of blood had soaked through part of the bandage. The sun beat down on him, causing perspiration to pool around his neck.

"I was shot."

"Seriously?" he asked, sounding as if there had been some kind of trophy involved. His driver turned onto the next channel. "So have you ever shot anyone?"

Joe ignored the question. Kept his eyes straight ahead. It had to be Anna who'd shot him. And now Anna had taken Talia. Did she really think she could simply grab Talia and vanish? But Talia had been right about her assessment. Anna was running scared, trapped with few options, if she wanted to get her hands on the paintings.

"Can you still see her?" Joe asked.

He searched the narrow canal as they turned the corner. Buildings rose up beside them from the murky waters, with their exposed brick walls and green moss along the water line. Arched doorways, old bridges with wrought-iron rails, a row of gondolas dipped on the water line... But he could only focus on one thing. Talia. And if he lost her now he'd never forgive himself.

He caught sight of the next boat a hundred feet ahead at the next turn.

"Go left," he ordered.

"I see her. Who is she? A girlfriend...your wife?"

"She's—she's just a friend."

Crazy how a couple days ago, Talia hadn't even been that. She'd been nothing more than a complete stranger. Someone he'd approached because he had an alternative agenda. He wanted to find his brother's killer, and she happened to be his one lead to do just that. And yet now...no matter how many times he told himself not to get involved—that this was just another case—he couldn't stop thinking about her. And now he'd somehow let her slip away and let that woman grab her.

She'd felt guilt over Marco's death. Now he was feeling the same. Because somehow over the course of the past few days, anything he'd felt had only deepened. She'd somehow managed to walk into his life and turned it on end. She'd made him smile, made him laugh and made him want to protect her from everything that was going on around them. Made him want to take a chance at falling in love again.

If he was given that chance again.

"How do you know her?" the other man asked.

"It's a long story, and confidential," Joe added to keep the man off his back.

"So, what...if you told me you'd have to kill me?" The man laughed at his own lame joke.

"Something like that."

"I'm Silvio Gabriello, by the way."

"Agent Joe Bryant."

Joe stood up in the boat, searching as far as he could see, but with the heavy boat traffic, it was becoming harder to keep up.

"Do you see the boat?" He glanced down a narrow canal, where Anna could have pulled off if she thought she was being followed. There were dozens of the small veins of water. Dozens of places where she could dock and escape.

"Wait a minute…I see it now," Silvio said. "They're just ahead of that second *vaporetto*."

Joe moved to the other side of the boat. Bingo.

He glanced at his pilot. "We can't lose them again."

If Anna hadn't found the paintings then where would she go? She couldn't go back to the crime scene. The police would already have blocked off the Morello house. Which meant if the paintings were still there, getting access would be next to impossible.

"Where do you think she's going?" Joe asked.

"My guess is that they're heading toward one of the smaller, underpopulated islands. Which would be smart if you wanted to disappear, though I suppose it would be hard not to stand out. Especially if you didn't speak Italian. And on top of that there aren't many hotels to hole up in. You mainly have fishermen who are out at night, then take their catch to the wholesale fish market."

"Stay back, then. Close enough to where we

can see where they're going, but far enough back that she won't notice us."

Silvio nodded and moved into position, keeping a larger cargo boat between them.

"A bunch of friends and I sometimes hang out on one of the other islands. There are local bars and pizzerias, gardens, antique markets and vineyards. Most of them you won't find many tourists. Especially on San Michele."

"Why is that?"

"It's been the city's cemetery for over two hundred years. The only thing you'll find there are churches and long rows of tombs. So unless you have an interest for wandering around endless sections of graves with photos of the deceased in their Sunday best, there's not much reason to go there. Though in November, there is a pilgrimage to these graves every year to lay flowers—"

"Fascinating," Joe interrupted, not interested in his commentary. "Do you carry a weapon?"

"Yeah, I have a gun. Do you think you're going to need one?"

"It's possible, though I'm surprised you have one. I understand that private gun ownership isn't guaranteed in Italy by law."

"It's not. But I transport goods on the islands. And sometimes the things I transport are pretty pricy. It's all on the up-and-up and legal."

"That's good, because I can assure you that the woman we're after isn't following the law."

"What has she done?"

"Killed at least two people. And now kidnapped a third."

Silvio's face paled. "Why?"

"She wants something worth a couple million dollars."

"Don't you think we should call the police?"

"We don't exactly have time, and I'm not willing to spook her."

Silvio pulled a handgun out of a locked box. "So what am I supposed to do?"

"You said you wanted to be an agent," Joe said, hoping he didn't regret his decision. "You're now my backup."

"Ahh...like Crockett and Tubbs."

"Who?"

"Didn't you ever watch *Miami Vice*?" Silvio asked, keeping his gaze straight ahead. "Two undercover cops trying to stop the drug trade...I watch a lot of American reruns."

Joe frowned. "Just try not to actually shoot anyone."

FIFTEEN

Talia opened her eyes, then squinted into the bright sun. She was hot, her temples were pounding and her hands tied behind her back. She glanced around her as snippets of memories surfaced. Joe had gone to get her something to drink, then someone had grabbed her. She remembered the boat. Remembered being hit with a gun.

Anna.

She turned toward the helm. The woman she'd once trusted was steering the boat into the open waters. Away from Venice. Away from Joe.

"Did you kill Thomas?" Talia asked, loud enough to ensure she heard her over the strong winds.

Anna glanced back at her. "You're finally awake."

"Did you kill him?" she repeated.

"You want answers? Here's one. I honestly never set out to hurt Thomas."

Talia frowned. Intentions held no meaning at this point. "Tell me what happened that night. You at least owe me that."

Anna shrugged. "I don't owe you anything."

"If you killed my husband, you owe me the truth about his death."

"You always did ask too many questions." Anna pulled back her wind-blown hair and tied it up with a band. "The truth is that I had too many credit card bills. Student-loan over-due notices. Medical bills from my mother's illness. Thousands and thousands of dollars. So I started stealing evidence collected during raids. It was easier than you'd think. It started with a pile of cash tucked in a drawer. No one noticed. I had a few contacts on the side, where I could quickly get rid of the drugs. Eventually I stumbled across the paintings. I knew some cartel members used art as collateral, so I knew I'd hit the jackpot."

There were more questions Talia wanted to ask. Had Thomas been involved? Had Anna been the one who'd pulled the trigger and ended his life? But instead she held her tongue and simply listened.

"Then that night—that night Thomas caught

me. I didn't have time to think things through. Not with the rest of the team searching the other half of the house. So I shot him."

"So was Thomas involved in the thefts or did you set him up?"

"Does it really matter anymore? The money was good, but the paintings were going to be my way out. Then somehow in the chaos of that night, they went missing."

Talia stared at the horizon. They were approaching one of the outlying islands. "You're not answering my questions about Thomas. Did Thomas know what you were doing? Was he involved in the thefts?"

Anna hesitated before answering. "No. He had no idea what I was doing."

Talia tried to stop the swell of emotions. All this time she'd thought he'd betrayed her. "Why kill him?"

"Because Thomas was always so…black and white. He thought he could save the world. And when he found out what I was doing, he thought he could save me. The problem is I'm not exactly worth saving. So framing him became easier than giving myself up. I made sure that the case was quickly buried, and it managed to stay that way until your FBI friend decided to open it up again. I knew the truth was going to come out eventually, so I made a plan to disappear."

"But in order to leave the country, you needed the money from the paintings."

"I told you I never planned to hurt Thomas, but that night, when he discovered what I was doing... I didn't have a choice."

"You always had a choice."

The jagged pieces of the puzzle were finally coming together. Had she really been so wrong about Thomas? She'd believed he was guilty. That her own taste in men was skewed because she hadn't seen the truth. And yet he'd actually been the honorable man she'd once believed him to be, and had died trying to help his partner. Talia stared out at the water. If she died, no one would ever know that truth. Because she knew Anna had no intention of letting her go once this was over. Which was why giving up wasn't an option.

"Why did you kill his brother?" she asked, searching for more answers.

"Thomas's brother was another unfortunate accident." Anna kept talking as if she hadn't heard what Talia had said. "For him, anyway. If he would have just told me where the paintings were, I wouldn't have had to hurt him."

Instead, she'd killed him.

Talia shifted in her seat, then winced as the plastic restraints gouged into her wrists. "Why now, after all these years? What made you start looking for them again?"

"For months after Thomas's death I tried tracking them down. You had signed off for the paintings in part of Thomas's things, so I searched your house and looked into everyone who'd been involved in the chain of evidence. But I still couldn't find them anywhere. I figured someone had made a mistake, or they'd been snatched along the way. So even though I kept looking, I never found them. Then your FBI agent made the connection between the gun and the drug dealers and the paintings, and I figured I was being given another chance."

"So what happens now?"

"I believe your in-laws know where they are. And you're my leverage."

"And after you get what you want, then what? You're planning to kill me as well?"

"Well, I can't exactly leave a witness, now can I?" She chuckled as they approached one of the islands. "I know what you're thinking. That your FBI agent will come to your rescue. But he won't. Not this time."

Talia watched one of the hundred plus islands came into view ahead of them. Most tourists never saw the series of islands that were scattered across the lagoon away from the historic center of Venice. She'd toured them once with a few friends, and while she'd always love the city of Venice, the outlining islands were full of traditional Venetian culture in the making for hundreds of years. They were full of fishing boats, vineyards and cathedrals. Museums and tucked-away hotels and restaurants. All without the throng of tourists clogging up the waterways.

Which was more than likely why Anna was bringing her here.

"Where are we going?" Talia asked, refusing to give in to the panic trying to edge its way through her.

"A little place where we can hole up for a few days. Isolated enough that you won't give me any trouble. Close enough to the main islands that I can finish what I need to."

"And you think your plan will work?"

"Enough of your questions. And don't forget the rules. Don't even try to get the attention of any of the other boats."

Talia glanced behind them. There was another larger boat coming up behind them on their starboard side, along with a few scattered smaller boats. But none of them were coming to her rescue. Joe would have no idea where she was. No idea how to rescue her. Which meant she was on her own this time. And was why she had to come up with a plan.

Joe's muscles tensed as Silvio maneuvered his boat toward an empty space along the dock of one of Venice's outlying islands. He crouched on the bow, making sure to stay hidden behind the larger craft bobbing in the water between their boat and the craft Anna was just now docking. But as far as he could tell, Anna had no idea he was less than ten yards away. He caught a glimpse of Talia before they slid into the dock. She was sitting beneath the canopy, and looked as if her hands were secured behind her.

Anna started tying the line to the mooring pole. Joe nodded at Silvio, praying their impromptu plan worked. Silvio jumped onto the dock, carrying with him a map of the area, then quickly approached Anna's boat.

"Excuse me… Sorry to bother you." Silvio pulled open his map and started talking to Anna. "I'm a bit lost. I thought this was Sant'Erasmo, but now that I've docked, I'm not so sure."

Joe quickly jumped onto the larger cargo

boat beside them, then made his way around the stern, to where Anna was holding Talia.

"I think you're on the wrong island," Anna said. "But I'm just sightseeing, as well. I suggest you speak with one of the locals."

She started to turn back, but Silvio kept talking. "I'm visiting from down south. I've heard they grow the most incredible produce here—asparagus, purple artichokes. But now in looking at this map, I'm not sure." He flipped the map upside down.

"I said I can't help you," Anna said, raising her voice. "I'm sorry."

Time was running out. He was going to have to make his move. The boat rocked beneath Joe as he stepped onto the small, flat-bottomed *topetta*. Talia turned to him, eyes wide with surprise as he moved past her. He motioned at her to stay quiet, then quickly moved along the edge of the boat, to where Anna stood. She had a small handgun in a holster at the small of her back.

He came at her from behind, taking her by surprise. With one fluid motion, he disarmed her before tossing the weapon into the water.

"Two can play the same game," he said, twisting her arm behind her to restrain her.

But Anna wasn't going down without a fight.

She turned sharply and jammed her elbow into his injured arm. He took a step back, trying not to give in to the excruciating pain that shot through his body.

Talia rushed toward Anna to stop her, but constricted by her bound hands, she couldn't avoid Anna's disarming punch to the side of her face. Joe came back at her. This time he anticipated her next move and struck back. Anna landed with her face down on the deck and Joe's foot firmly planted against her back.

"Joe!"

Joe turned as Talia lost her balance and the momentum swung her over the edge of the boat and into the water. She hit the murky water headfirst.

"Keep your gun aimed on this woman," Joe shouted at Silvio, then jumped into the water after Talia.

He had no idea where she was. All he could see were particles of dirt floating around him. He started praying again as he searched the water. His eyes burned. His arm throbbed. But she was here somewhere. He found her struggling to get to the surface with her hands tied behind her. Grabbing her around the waist, he started for the surface, but she started fighting back. Joe held on to her tighter. His heart pounded as they broke the surface of the water. She gasped for air, and he caught the panic in her eyes.

"Talia, it's me. Stop. You're okay."

He held on to her tightly with his good arm, her chest heaving as she drew in another lungful of air. He managed to pull her up onto the dock then laid her down carefully on her back. He grabbed his pocketknife then snapped off the restraint.

"Talia…" He hovered beside her where she lay, still trying to catch her breath. "Please tell me you're okay."

Despite the hot sun pounding down on her, her body was shaking. A mixture, he was sure, of both fear and relief.

"Talia? Are you okay?"

She managed a nod.

"Try to breathe, then. Slow, deep breaths."

"Where's Anna?" she asked.

"She's still on the boat, but you're safe. She's not going to be able to hurt you anymore."

Talia turned her head toward the boat. Silvio still stood on the stern, pointing his gun at Anna. "Who is he?"

"Agent Silvio Gabriello," Joe said, turning to his new friend. "And someone I owe a debt of gratitude."

"That 'agent' bit might just grow on me," Silvio said, not taking his eyes off Anna. "In case you were wondering, we just needed a distraction," he said to her. "I know this island very well. In fact, I have a number of friends who live here. A few burly fishermen. I gave them a call as we were pulling up to the dock. They're on their way here now to ensure you are placed in custody until the *polizia* show up."

"I still don't understand who he is," Talia said.

"I'll tell you all about him later. Do you think you can sit up?"

Talia pressed her hands against him and managed to sit up. Her dark hair clung to her face, where a nasty bruise was beginning to show up. But at least she was alive and safe.

She scrunched her hair with her fingers, then turned back to Joe, her gaze stopping at his arm, where he'd been shot the day before. She reached up and pulled at his sleeve. "Your arm…it's bleeding again."

"Forget about my arm. It will be fine. I was afraid I'd lost you out there."

"How in the world did you find me?"

He shot her a smile. "I have a few resources available to me."

"She was going to kill me as soon as she got those paintings."

"I know, and I couldn't let that happen."

"She was planning to use me as leverage."

"So she never found the paintings."

"No. And there's another thing I found out. Thomas was innocent."

"Innocent? What do you mean?"

"Thomas never should have died. She framed him. She was the one stealing from the raids, and he found out. She ended up killing him and planting evidence on him."

He wiped away the water running down her cheek. She had to be exhausted both physically and emotionally. But now, while nothing was going to bring Thomas back, maybe she could move on with her life knowing he really had been the man she'd always believed he was.

"I'm so sorry for everything you've had to go through," he said.

"So am I, but it's over, Joe. And I finally know the truth."

He could hear the relief in her voice, but it wasn't over. Not completely. Not for him. He glanced at Anna. There was still a connection between Anna, the paintings and the murder weapon that killed both Thomas and his brother, and he intended to find it.

SIXTEEN

Joe stood in the doorway of the Morellos' living room that led onto the balcony of the small apartment. He watched Talia interact with friends and family. It looked as if most of the neighborhood had shown up and were now pressed into the small space. Rows of food in covered dishes sat on the counters of the adjacent kitchen, leaving the place smelling like garlic, onions and tomatoes. He was reminded that he couldn't remember the last time he'd eaten.

But eating seemed almost frivolous.

He could read a hint of pain in her eyes as Talia stood talking to an older woman. He'd spent the past thirty-six hours visiting the local doctor to make sure his wound wasn't getting infected, then sleeping off the pain medicine.

Now, two days later, the police had finally finished with their closed crime scene, giving the family back a semblance of normality. But things would never be the same. And the hardest part of all, in his mind, was the fact that the loss of the Morellos' children had been completely senseless. Even with Anna locked behind bars for the rest of her life, it would never be enough to make up for the pain and loss they'd experienced.

Talia greeted another neighbor with a solemn expression, then started toward him. He'd debated coming at all. She'd spent the day before with her in-laws, trying to help them make sense of everything that had happened. He should have left and yet something had kept him from going. Maybe it was his own sense of needing closure. Or maybe it was the woman walking toward him that he wasn't quite ready to leave.

He worried about how she was handling things, and the memories this entire experience had triggered. And yet at the same time he'd been impressed with how strong she was. How she hadn't allowed fear to stop her from standing tall when conflict struck. It was what had drawn him to her in the first place. A mixture of vulnerability and strength.

Which was partly why he was still standing here. That not-so-subtle desire to get to know her had refused to leave no matter how hard he tried to ignore it. He hadn't been looking—wasn't looking—and yet he knew that she was the kind of woman, given time, that he'd like to spend the rest of his life with.

She stopped in front of him, looking beautiful in a black-and-white dress that dropped just above a pair of silver sandals. But it was her smile that had his heart in a tailspin.

"Hey, " he said, stepping out onto the balcony with her. "How are you doing?"

"I've had better days, but I'm okay. I'm glad you're here. I could use a bit of air."

Outside on the balcony gave them a mesmerizing view of the canal. While he'd never tire of the city scene, Venice would always be more than just a tourist stop for him.

"I know this hasn't been an easy few days," he said, keeping his thoughts focused.

"To be honest I've had worse days. And this time I'm not the one facing the brunt of the loss. But I'm sorry to have left you to fend for yourself after you brought me here."

"You have nothing to apologize for. I'm just glad you're here with Marco's parents. They need you."

"It's been good, though, just to get to chat with some Marco's friends and family. It's been so long since I've seen many of them. I just wish I wasn't here because of his death. It still seems so surreal."

"And you? How are you being here? I know it had to have brought a lot of difficult memories back to the surface."

"It has, but it's also been good for me to be here. I've known many of these people for years. Even before Thomas and I were married. It's always a bit like coming home, and yet at the same time everything seems so different. So much has happened since then. Babies born, people who have passed away…"

He studied her face as she stared out over the canal. She'd given her heart to two countries and loved them both deeply.

"You look tired," he said.

"I am. But it's my in-laws I'm worried about. They're strong, but they've lost so much. First Thomas and now Marco."

"I can't imagine what they are going through."

"Me neither, though they seem…I guess *shattered* is the right word. In the meantime, there is family here. A sister and a niece who are going to stay with them for a while. And they have the entire community behind them."

"And you're here," he added.

"Yes, but I think it's hard for them when I'm

here. They care about me, I have no doubt of that, but I think I'm a reminder of what they've lost. I'm not sure how long I should stay. Not sure if they need me."

He glanced out beyond the balcony. "You said you needed some fresh air. Do you feel like going for a walk? There's something I'd like to show you."

She looked up at him and nodded. "Actually...I would."

"Good."

They stepped outside into the humid summer breeze and started down the narrow street toward the canal. Past a few restaurants and bars with customers sitting out in front of them drinking coffee and laughing. He'd always found it ironic how the world still went on around you even when your own world seemed to be ending.

Like the day his brother died.

He was still waiting, but maybe with the new information they now had, he'd also be able to find closure for himself and his family. And for Talia... All he could do was pray that she felt the same way. That as difficult as the past few days had been, that she'd find healing and a way forward.

"Are you up for a surprise?" he asked, as he headed toward the canal.

"A surprise?" She frowned, making him wonder if he'd misread her.

"Don't worry. It's a good thing." He hesitated. "You said you'd never gone on gondola. I met a friend of yours and mentioned that I'd like to take one of them one day. He offered to take us. You can say no, but I thought you might like to get out of the house for a while."

"A gondola ride?" She still didn't look convinced. "Are you serious?"

"Very. But too touristy?"

"Yes." She laughed. The first laugh he'd heard from her in days. "But it's perfect, actually. I could use a distraction. And they don't need me back anytime soon."

He smiled at her. "I was hoping you'd say that."

He led her down to the gondola, where the man he'd hired, wearing a black-and-white striped shirt and black pants, waited for them. Before long the sun would begin to set, giving them a front row seat to a perfect Venetian sunset.

"Bruno?" she said, stepping into the boat. "I haven't seen you for a long time. It's nice to see you."

"It's nice to you, too, though I can't believe you've never taken a ride in a gondola before. I would have thought you'd given a tour on one if nothing else."

"I'm too much of a local, preferring to walk or take the *vaporetto*."

Her smile was back, as he helped her onto the boat, leaving him with a feeling that he'd made the right decision.

"I have to say that this city continues to amaze me," he said, settling into the boat. "And the view from the water—especially when I'm not chasing someone—is spectacular."

The boat glided down the narrow passageway, next to century-old buildings rising out of its depths.

She leaned in next to him. "I never get tired of the water or the views of the city or being out on the water. There something mesmerizing about it."

He studied the gondola ahead of them as it navigated the canals. "Look at them. I think I should have added the accordion player and singer."

"No. This is perfect." She nudged him with her shoulder as the music played. "Though I remember someone telling me they'd learned not to mix business with pleasure."

"Maybe I was wrong."

He looked down at her, contemplating whether or not he should put his arm around her, and let her lean even closer against him. Because he wanted to. Wanted to reassure himself that she was safe. Except a part of him wished it didn't feel so perfect for her to be next to him. He was leaving in the morning. He'd already booked a train ticket to Rome and had a flight out in the evening. And after he was gone…

The setting sun painted yellows and pinks across the water and buildings. Bells from the Venetian Basilica rang out across the Grand Canal. Boats sped past them with their passengers. No roads. Nothing to really think about for the moment, except the movement of the water and the beautiful woman sitting beside him.

Because she was nothing like Natasha.

He'd only mentioned Natasha to a few people. And he'd never told them what had really happened. He'd just stopped talking about her, and yet there was something about Talia that made it easy for him to open up. Something completely unexpected.

"Her name was Natasha Waybright," he said, deciding to tell her the truth.

"You don't have to tell me," she said.

"I know, but I need to. She worked for an upscale art gallery, primarily for contemporary artists. She ended up helping us with a sting operation we were working in connection to a number of art-fraud cases we needed to close down. It was supposed to be straightforward, but things didn't exactly go as planned."

"What happened?"

"Turned out our intel was off. Way off. The owner wasn't the one involved in the scam. It was Natasha all along."

"So she played you."

"Like a fiddle. And let me tell you, that admission still hurts."

"I'm so sorry."

"It embarrassing for our team."

Particularly for him, someone who prided himself on being able to read people. It had been a blow to both his ego and his heart.

"She's now spending ten to fifteen behind bars," he said. "And let's just say that after that, I learned to keep my job completely separate from my private life."

"I've always found dating—especially after Thomas—a bit... I'm not sure what the word is. *Awkward, intimidating* and even *unnerving*, for starters."

Joe laughed. "I once heard dating compared to jumping into a tank of piranhas."

"I can relate to that." She shot him a smile as a boat sped past them. "I ended up having to feign a headache and walk out on my last date after watching him constantly texting someone else throughout the entire appetizer."

"That is bad."

"Not quite as bad as you falling for a criminal, but yeah. It wasn't pleasant." Her smile faded. "I believed Thomas had fooled me, as well. And sometimes I'm not sure it's something I can get past. Though my heart tells me that not all people are like Natasha. There are some out there who are simply looking for love, marriage and a family."

Talia glanced up at him. "Thanks for sharing with me. And I meant what I said. This is perfect."

He smiled down at her, but he knew he was treading on dangerous territory. She'd stay for a few more days, then head back to Rome, but he was leaving Italy, and after that…what chance did they have that their paths would cross again?

She glanced up at him and smiled, wishing his nearness didn't affect her, but it did. Over a matter of days, Agent Joe Bryant had somehow managed to become her hero, her rock, her spiritual adviser and friend all rolled up into one.

"Thank you for this."

He smiled back. "You're welcome."

"I have to say that while all of the loose ends weren't exactly tied up in a neat bow like I would have wished, this is the first time I've been able to relax for days."

"That's exactly what I'd hoped for."

She stared out across the water at the spectacular sunset, still hoping they would find the paintings and even more importantly hoped that Joe would find the closure he needed regarding his brother's death. She'd somehow managed to find that lingering need for closure with Anna's confession. And while the truth had pulled open old wounds, in the end, she knew they would now finally be able to heal.

"I've learned something these past few days," she said.

"What's that?"

"That maybe my taste in men maybe isn't so bad after all."

He nudged her with his elbow. "If you're referring to me, I happen to know that your taste in men is impeccable."

"Funny."

She'd meant Thomas, but had she subconsciously meant Joe as well? Because while she might feel the attraction toward him, that didn't mean she was ready to move into another relationship. Or was she?

She looked up at him, suddenly questioning whether she should have agreed to come with him. The setting was too…perfect. Too romantic. Gliding down the Grand Canal in a shiny black gondola in the middle of Venice with him. The sun had slipped farther toward the horizon and now was in the process of bathing the buildings and water in pinks and purples, with Joe, the handsome agent who'd come to her rescue, beside her.

He was what she was looking for. If she was looking. The bigger-than-life hero with a heart and passion for what he did. But wasn't it just that for him? Another job? The intensity of the past few days wasn't real life. It might be a start, but it wasn't something to build a relationship on. And after tomorrow she'd go back to the real world, and he'd go back to his.

"I know that these past few days have been extremely difficult," he said, breaking into her thoughts. "It definitely hasn't been the kind of situation that allows two people to get to know each other in a real world setting. But tell me something. Tell me I haven't just imagined a connection between us."

"I… No. You haven't, but…" She looked up at him and felt her breath catch.

Maybe it was the fading sunlight playing hide-and-seek as it dropped behind a building, leaving a shadow of gold shimmering across the water. Maybe it was the black silhouette of another gondola gliding ahead of them. The perfect romantic scene. The perfect hero sitting beside her. He'd saved her life, but in the process he'd also managed to do something to her heart. Like he'd found all the vulnerable cracks and instead of breaking them, he'd managed to soften them.

Fear that had threatened to consume her moments before dissipated. He leaned toward her and she let him brush her lips across hers. Her heart raced as he kissed her, slowly, expectantly, with the Venetian sun dipping into the dark waters in front of them. Seconds later, she pulled back, unsure of what she'd just done.

"I'm sorry," he said. "That was…out of line. Between knowing me for such a short time, and the loss of your husband—"

"It's not that. I've healed over losing Thomas. That doesn't mean there aren't still things that trigger memories and feelings of grief that sometimes linger, but I'm not in that place anymore. To be honest, this past week has been one of the most frightening times I've ever experienced, and yet it's also reminded me of how far I've come. How I'm a stronger person than I used to be. I don't know if I'd have been able to handle what happened two... maybe three years ago. But exploring a relationship?" She let out a low laugh. Part of her wanted to run, but the other part of her wanted him to kiss her again. "I'll be honest, I don't know if it's me or the men I've gone out with, but typically I never get to a second date."

"What are you looking for?"

His question caught her off guard. How many times had she sat around eating her favorite triple-fudge ice cream with extra fudge sauce and whipped cream while her sister asked her the same question?

What was she looking for?

She looked up at Joe and caught his gaze. Her heart tripped, something that was becoming a far too common response to being around him.

"I know we've only known each other a short time," he said, not waiting for an answer. "But I'd like to get to know you better, Talia. See if it's possible for something to continue between us. Have you thought about that at all?"

She felt a blush cross her cheeks. "You told me you learned not to mix business with pleasure."

"That was before I met you."

"I live in Italy," she said. "You live in the States."

"There is Skype, email and frequent flyer points."

She was throwing out excuses and she knew it, but there was something else. Something she was really afraid to look at.

"What is it?" he asked.

"There is something else." She hesitated while darkness began to settle over the city. "Everything that happened—your getting shot, me being kidnapped by Anna—that is your life. Not mine. You're used to chasing down the bad guys, having your adrenaline pumping, but that's not my life. And I don't want that to be my life."

"What do you mean?"

"Believing Thomas wasn't the person I thought he was for all these years isn't my only hesitation for not moving into another relationship."

"Then what is?"

"I was married to a police officer. He went out risking his life every day for his community. I never knew if he was going to come home to me at night. Could never completely relax until he walked through that door after his shift, and I knew for sure he was okay."

Talia paused. Was that the real issue? The fact that she'd been afraid of losing Thomas and when she did...

"One day, all my fears were realized when he didn't walk through that door. I don't want to go through that again."

Joe shifted beside her while their gondola sliced across the water. "Do you regret your life with Thomas?"

She shook her head. "Now that I know he really was the man I thought he was I don't regret it. I wish there had been a happier ending, but no."

"If you had known what was going to happen when you'd married him, would you have still gone through with it, or tried to avoid the pain that comes with loss?"

She stared at the lights reflecting across the water and up the walls of the city, wishing he wouldn't ask such probing questions. Water lapped against the sides of the boat. The dark waters were now lit from the lights lining the canal. Everyone knew the saying that it was better to have loved and lost then to have never have loved at all. And it was true. Or at least she thought it was true. But was she willing to make that same decision again?

Their boat passed an open window, where a couple stood on their balcony drinking from fluted glasses. A brightly lit chandelier glowed inside the background of the apartment.

"I don't know," she said finally.

"Fair enough, but none of us know the future. We don't know what's going to happen to us tomorrow, let alone today. Just don't base your decisions on fear. You don't know what you might miss out on in the meantime."

He knew she was right. But did she have enough strength to step out and try love again?

Water lapped against the sides of the boat as Bruno pushed them down the canal. It was a place that had brought her to the point of feeling happy again. A place where she'd finally found peace.

"Talia?"

"Sorry. I was just lost in thought."

"You once told me that your stint in Rome was temporary. If you could do anything you wanted career-wise moving forward, what would you do?"

He was changing the subject. Trying to diminish any awkwardness that had settled between them. "I'd like to teach art again. I stepped away from it after Thomas died."

"I've said it before, but I'd still like to see some of your paintings."

"You have, actually."

"I have? Where?"

"At my in-laws' place. Do you remember the painting of Venice at sunrise hanging next to the bookshelf in their living room?"

"That was yours?"

She nodded.

"You're good, Talia. Good enough to have your paintings in a gallery."

"I don't ever plan on selling them, but it's something I enjoy."

She caught his gaze, wondering how long she'd gone without really living. He'd reminded her of things that had once brought her joy. And with it there was something steady and solid about him that left her feeling safe and secure. As if a part of her was coming back to life again.

The boat bobbed beneath them as they glided back toward the dock and a long line of gondolas. While she still wasn't ready for her heart to make a decision, tonight had helped to bring things back into perspective for her. To remind her what it was like to live again. And to maybe let her heart feel again.

She took his hand and laced their fingers together. "Thank you."

"You're welcome. And I hope this won't be your last gondola ride."

"Somehow I don't think it will be." Bruno eased the sleek boat next to the dock. "Can you imagine that two hundred years ago, there were ten thousand gondolas navigating the shifting sandbars of the canals?"

"Ten thousand? And today?"

"Today there are only four hundred, and while everyone uses boats for their mode of transportation, the gondolas are only for the tourists. The locals typically have their own recreational boats."

A memory snapped to the forefront.

Most weekends, when Marco wasn't working, he headed to the surrounding islands that most tourists had yet to discover. Once he'd invited her and Thomas along on a friend's boat to a long stretch of quiet beaches. Before the sun set, they'd visited a small fisherman's village, with their brightly painted cottages and fishing boats, where they'd stuffed themselves on seafood and crepes filled with baby artichokes.

She ran her fingers across the edge of the gondola. Marco used a boat to transport goods to local shops throughout the week, and she knew that the police had searched that boat. But no one had found the paintings. Not there, or in Marco's apartment, or in the Morello home.

But they knew that Marco had the paintings and that Anna hadn't found them. And a boat, on an island filled with thousands of them, would be the perfect hiding place.

"Joe…"

"What is it?"

She glanced up at him. "I think I might know where the paintings are."

SEVENTEEN

Talia waited until they'd left the gondola behind, bobbing in the darkened waters of the canal, before she said anything else. "You know, I might be simply grasping at straws with this."

"So what are you thinking?" Joe asked.

"We both know that Marco spent his days working here in Venice, but on the weekends, he normally headed out with friends. One of them has a boat they take out to hang out on some of the quieter islands. A lot of the locals do the same thing."

They headed back through a maze of narrow streets toward the Morellos' apartment. Maybe she was way off, but on the other hand, maybe it was worth looking at.

"When I spoke to him last," she continued, "he mentioned he was going out with one of his friends on his boat."

"Whose boat?"

"A guy by the name of Celso. I'm not sure about his last name, I only met him a couple times. And I know it's a long shot, but we know Marco had the paintings. We know Anna didn't find them. The police have searched and haven't been able to find them, either, but they have to be somewhere."

"I think it's worth looking at. But at this point it seems like they could be anywhere."

"It's funny," she said as they kept walking. "I didn't think I cared about finding them. In fact I didn't want anything to do with those paintings, but now—but now they seem like one of the final pieces of the puzzle that need to be put into place, I think because if they're found, no one will attempt linking them back to me."

She breathed in a deep breath and felt herself relaxing again. Feeling safe again with him beside her. The hot July temperatures had cooled significantly, partly thanks to the breezes of the lagoon. The city was also quieter after the sunset. After the throngs of tourists had left the city to go back to their cruise ships, beachside resorts and the cheaper hotels on the mainland. In their place, she could hear the melodic strains of an orchestra playing beneath the full moon somewhere near St. Mark's Square.

She glanced up at Joe's solid profile. She knew he was still waiting for answers about his brother. With Anna now in police custody, they were expecting answers from her. But for the moment, she realized all she really wanted to do was prolong their evening together. Before Joe left Italy and her world went back to normal.

If life ever could really be normal again.

At six the next morning, with the sun barely up above the horizon, Talia stepped onto Celso Amato's boat, which was docked along a quiet vein of the city's canal. After a few phone calls last night, she'd been able to contact Marco's friend, who'd quickly passed on his condolences, then agreed to let them come get Marco's things, as she'd put it.

She was glad Celso had agreed to meet them early. In a few more hours, the heat would feel relentless again. She stood at the stern and studied the forty-foot boat, wondering if she was off with her conclusion. There weren't a lot of places to hide things beyond the cabin and the limited storage areas. She'd spoken to Marco's parents again last night. They had told

Marco she was coming to look for a collection of paintings. The last message they'd received from him was that he'd found them and planned to have them appraised.

They'd never heard from him again.

"I still can't believe he's gone," Celso said.

Talia turned to Marco's friend, who stood in the middle of the deck. "I can't, either."

"We hung out this past weekend. Spent all of Saturday away from the crowds. Went to dinner with friends Monday night." Celso shoved his hands into his front pockets while Joe started looking through the cabin. "I'm not sure what you're looking for, but Marco was always leaving stuff on the boat. Sunglasses, hats, his keys—you name it."

"We're looking for some paintings Marco had."

"Can't say that I ever saw anything like that." Celso shrugged. "But I'll leave you to your search. I'm supposed to meet someone in a few minutes."

Talia glanced at Joe, then decided to start at the helm. There were two things she didn't want to think about as she searched. One was the fact that Joe was leaving in a few hours to return to the US. Two was what if they didn't find the paintings? Somehow both mattered.

"Anything?" Joe asked a few minutes later.

"Not yet."

"I'd hoped your idea would come through, but I don't think they're here, Talia"

"I'm afraid I might have to agree with you." She finished searching a small storage space near the bow. Nothing. "Wait a minute."

"What have you got?"

Something was taped beneath the bench. She pulled out a yellow envelope from inside a sealed plastic bag.

Talia sat down on the bench and slid out the contents.

The three paintings.

"You were right," he said, picking up one of them.

She took in the even strokes and pastel colors. "I remember them. They're beautiful. I just never imagined they would be worth so much or cause so many problems."

"This case was a bit like opening Pandora's box, but it's over now."

Relief swept through her. Having Joe with her made her feel safe again. She glanced up to where he stood with the Grand Canal behind him. He made her feel as if she could actually start over again with someone else.

Which was what she wanted. Wasn't it? But

was Joe the right person? Or had everything that had happened between them been nothing more than a reaction to what they'd been through over the past week?

"While they are beautiful, I don't want anything to do with them." She handed them to Joe. "Not after all the trouble they've caused."

"I don't blame you, but somehow I don't think the artist who drew these could ever have imagined the lives they were going to affect one day."

"Which is why we're going to ensure that they go back to the museum, where they belong—"

"Not so fast." An armed man stepped onto the boat and aimed his gun at Talia and the paintings. "I'll take those off your hands now."

Joe quickly moved between Talia and the gunman. "What do you want?"

"Those paintings Ms. Morello's holding, for starters."

"Why? Who are you?" Joe stood his ground.

"Captain Blythe," Talia said, standing up behind him. "I'm guessing you were in on this cover-up with Anna all along. Stealing evidence from the raids...my husband's murder."

"I had nothing to do with the death of your husband."

"But you knew Anna killed him, and I'm assuming you were also happy to keep your take of the spoils while keeping your mouth shut. Is that how it worked? It's the only explanation that makes sense to me as to why you're here wanting these paintings."

"Which must mean that Anna double-crossed you," Joe added.

The tension in the air was palpable. The boat bobbed beneath them. Joe steadied himself in front of the other man.

"She came to Italy to ensure you didn't start asking another slew of questions now that the case has been reopened," Blythe finally answered. "The last thing we needed was for you and now Mr. FBI here to start poking around and discover the holes in your husband's case. Anything that could point to me. I couldn't exactly let you get a hold of that type of evidence."

"Looks like you trusted the wrong person when it came to Anna. Especially since she's probably telling the local police all about you."

"It doesn't matter now. I'll take those paintings and be the one to live out the rest of my life on some tropical island. Beats prison."

Blythe shook his head. "I knew I should have taken you out back then. I was always worried you'd find out the truth."

"Which she has," Joe said. "We both have."

"So what happens now?" Talia asked.

"Start the motor. We'll be going for a bit of a ride. You'll be the driver, Talia. I'm assuming you learned something about boats from all your time here in Venice, and don't try anything or your boyfriend here will be the first one overboard."

"You really think this plan will work?" Joe asked.

"We're pretty isolated here, and I don't see anyone stopping us. Talia, hand me the paintings. Just in case you get any bright ideas."

She tossed them toward the captain and they landed on the deck a foot from his feet.

Joe took the distraction to grab the man's wrist with his good arm, then spun the barrel away from them in one fluid motion. With the gun out of play, he quickly flipped the man onto the deck. Blythe came down hard against a metal post.

"He's out cold. For now," Joe said, feeling a jolt of pain shoot through his injured arm. "Why don't you give the police a call while I tie him up with that rope?"

She nodded, then grabbed her phone.

"I trusted him," she said, once she'd finished the call.

"You okay?"

She nodded, but he could tell she was trembling. He wanted to pull her into his arms, but he had no idea how she would react. No idea where things stood between the two of them.

"You had no way of knowing he was dirty."

"I should have known that Anna couldn't have buried the case on her own. She needed someone higher up to bury the evidence and ensure Thomas was framed."

"It's over now, Talia."

"I hope so. I keep waiting for the next crisis to hit."

"And there will be another crisis at some point, because this is life. But I meant what I said on the boat. I think there's a chance for something between you and me and I'd like to find out. But it's up to you."

Sirens sounded in the background. In a few minutes, they'd arrest Blythe and it really would be over.

"I just need some time," she said, standing in the middle of the boat, clutching the paintings against her. "Not forever, but some time."

"I can give all the time you need." When

she didn't respond, he asked another question. "What are your plans after this? Going back to Rome?"

"For now. First I've got to figure out everything that happened this week and how it affects me."

"Okay." He wanted to say he understood, but he didn't. Not completely. He wanted to say that they could find a way to sort out living in two continents and figure out ways to get to know each other, but he knew that for the moment, the past still lay between them. "I'm leaving tonight unless you need me to stay."

The police boat turned into the narrow waterway behind them as Blythe started to stir. The loneliness he hadn't even realized he'd been feeling before he met her began to seep in.

She pressed her lips together. "Thank you. For everything."

"You're welcome. Just promise me one thing. That you'll keep in touch."

She smiled up at him, but he didn't miss the tears pooling in her eyes. "I will. I promise."

EIGHTEEN

Rome, six weeks later

Talia fell back onto the couch in her apartment, propped her feet up on the coffee table, then let out a sharp sigh of relief.

Carla, her Italian friend and coworker for the last three years, stood over her. "Oh, no, you don't. This is not how you're going to spend your evening off. Because when I suggested we hang out tonight, I didn't mean here in your living room."

"Why not? A movie and takeaway after a week of interacting with tourists sounds pretty perfect to me."

"Forget it. You've been moping around this apartment for the past month. It's time for you to get up off that couch and do something. We could go to the market at Campo de' Fiori, or drive up to Monte Mario, or there's a concert tonight—"

Talia frowned. Clearly her friend wasn't planning on letting her off the hook.

"Too touristy?" Carla asked.

"My feet hurt, and—"

"Seriously, girl, I think it's time for an intervention. All you do is work, then come home and stare at the television. You eat cereal for dinner and leftover pizza for breakfast. You barely go out with your friends, let alone on dates."

"Your point?"

"My point?" Talia caught the exasperation in her friend's voice as she spoke. "My point is that you need to snap out of it."

Except she wasn't quite sure how. Instead she was distracted, moody and barely had enough energy to get through her day, let alone go out again at night.

"I know what the problem is," Carla said, plopping down beside her.

"What?"

"It's that tall, dark and handsome FBI agent you haven't wanted to talk about since you returned."

"How I feel has nothing to do with Joe."

"Then why do I keep catching you staring

at that selfie you think I don't know about on your phone?"

Talia's frown deepened. "I've done that once…maybe twice."

"Right. And I know he calls you. Almost every day."

"So? He saved my life. We've been chatting. Talking on the phone. Messaging each other."

"Just be honest with me. Okay?" Carla pulled her legs up underneath her. "And if you won't be honest with me, at least be honest with yourself. Because I know the signs. You can't stop thinking about him. It affects your sleep and your eating—"

"Okay." Talia picked at a hangnail, wishing her friend's diagnosis wasn't so spot on. "What if I am in love with him? I'm afraid if I hand him my heart, I'll lose it, and I don't think I can do that again."

"Love's always a risk."

"But Thomas was a lawman. Joe's a lawman."

"I get the connection, but not the problem. He's not Thomas."

The reality of the situation wormed its way through her as she made an attempt to explain. "I loved another lawman who had a dangerous job. What happens if I let Joe into my life and lose him?"

"I'm sure you've heard this one before, but what happens if you let him into your life and don't lose him? Or what if you don't let him into your life and you never find out what could have been?"

Talia groaned. "Stop making so much sense."

"Why, because you're about to walk away from the best thing that's happened to you in a long time?"

She couldn't argue with her. Because everything she was saying did make sense. Falling in love again always seemed a bit like stepping off a cliff. And yet as sappy as it sounded, there was something about being with Joe that made her feel as if she could fly.

"He wants me to go back to the US," she said.

"Sounds romantic."

"I'm not sure that *romantic* is the word. The paintings are being donated to the museum. He thought I might like to be there. Thought it would help with the closure of everything that happened."

The nightmares had begun to fade. She no longer found herself jumping at every loud noise or constantly looking over her shoulder, as she had been. And she'd begun to look forward to Joe's calls, making the line between her desire to guard her heart and give it away begin to blur.

"If you went to the States, you'd get to see him," Carla said. "Isn't that what the trip would really be about? Besides, it's time you moved on with your life."

Talia closed her eyes and allowed a flow of memories to surface. The moment he'd come to her rescue outside the Colosseum, walking through Florence, sitting beside him in the gondola when he kissed her... If she was completely honest with herself, she wanted to see him again. Badly.

"I don't know if I'm ready," she said.

"You're ready," Carla said. "And it's time you followed your heart."

"On behalf of the Flinmore Gallery, we want to thank you for returning these paintings to their rightful owner..."

Joe tuned out the pale, lanky curator's detailed history of the Li Fonti paintings and how the museum originally came into possession of them. As far as he was concerned, their journey over the past couple years had been far more newsworthy. They'd been stolen from the museum, used as collateral for the drug trade and had eventually cost the lives of at least two people. He was glad they were out of his hands and back in their rightful place.

He just wished Talia could have been here to see it happen.

At the end of the curator's speech, the small crowd gathered around them gave a short round of applause, then silently dispersed.

A woman walked up to the display and stopped in front of the paintings next to where he stood. "I can't believe I missed the ceremony. Traffic from the airport was horrible."

"Talia?" Joe felt his heart catch as he heard the familiar voice.

"I still think they're beautiful, but I'm glad that they're here, out of my life, where hopefully no one can ever steal them again. Or at the least involve me."

"You came," he said, uncertain he wasn't dreaming.

"I wasn't sure I was going to. Not at first. But I thought seeing the paintings hanging on a museum wall would bring closure." She drew in a deep breath then caught his gaze. "And there's another reason I came. I missed you."

"I've missed you, too," he said, his mind

whirling with the implications of her presence. "You look…beautiful."

He caught the blush creep across her cheeks as she glanced down at the bright blue fabric of her dress swirling just above her ankles.

"Thanks."

"How long are you staying?"

"I'm not sure yet. I thought for starters we could spend the day together. If you're free."

"Of course." There were so many things he'd imagined showing her if she ever visited, but for the moment all he could think about was the fact that she was actually here. "Would you like to look around the museum for a few minutes first?"

"My only plan for today is to spend the day with you, but you know me. I can't exactly pass up a new museum."

He took her hand, enjoying watching her as much as the artwork. Over the last few weeks, he'd found himself waking up every morning hoping there was a message from her. Between the time change and their jobs, connecting had been a challenge. It usually meant him calling her before he went to bed and before she went to work in the morning.

But they'd managed to make it work. He'd laugh over something a tourist had said, while she'd worry about him when he told her he'd taken on a new case. She told him funny stories of trips to Europe with her parents, and how she'd gotten the scar on the back of her hand. How she hated broccoli and loved tapioca pudding. Preferred coffee over tea, and never passed up anything with frosting and sprinkles on it.

And now here he was, getting to spend the day with her. But the thing was, he'd already realized that he didn't just want to spend today with her, but every day. Text messages and phone calls weren't enough. And while part of him had no idea how to pull it off, he'd decided that any effort he had to put into making them work was going to be worth it.

"This room is stunning," she said.

"I thought you might like it. A few Italian masterpieces on the wall. Carlevarijs, Guercino, Li Fonti…"

"You've been doing your homework," she said.

"Just trying to impress you."

Talia laughed. "You don't have to try to impress me. You already do."

"There's something you need to know about the Li Fonti paintings," he said. "I got a call as I was arriving here in regards to my brother."

"You found out who killed him?"

"Anna confessed that the gun she used had been in the house and belonged to one of the drug dealers. We were able to finally get a hit on the fingerprints and connect them to the museum robbery. The two men believed to be involved were arrested earlier today."

"So it's really over now. For both of us."

Joe nodded. "And like you, I'm learning to put all of this in the past. But as for the present…" He hesitated before continuing. There were so many things he wanted to say to her. He just wasn't sure when it was going to be the right time. Or if another time would ever be better.

"I've been thinking a lot about my future," he said, finally.

"With the FBI?"

"More of a personal nature."

"Meaning?"

"I promised I'd give you time, and I meant that. I won't push you. But the last few weeks of getting to know you have only managed to convince me even more that I'd like to find a way to work around the different time zones and continents and see each other more. Like this."

She stopped in front of another painting and